SEAN M. T.

Only
The Damned
Can
Save Us

for Charlotte

NECROMANCING
THE ROSE

Book 1 of the
Whim-Dark Tales

Copyright © 2023 by Sean M. T. Shanahan – First Edition
All rights reserved. No part of this book may be reproduced or used in any manner without written permission of the copyright owner except for the use of quotations in a book review. For more information, address: sean@seanmts.com
First Edition
www.seanmts.com[1]
Edited by the Ebook Launch Team.
Cover design by Miblart.

---

1. http://www.seanmts.com

Part I: The Puppet Master Druid

It was a dark night.

Lingering smoke clung to the skies like a caustic rash, spreading coarse, suffocating fumes across the land. The woods were a smouldering skeleton blanketed in grey and black ash, which dampened the footsteps of two hunters, one stalking the other.

Gazlan trudged and stumbled through the inferno's wake. His usual gliding gait was hobbled by exposed gnarled roots, collapsing soil, and the littered carcasses of the dead. It didn't help that he could hardly see the corporeal world in these conditions. He pulled his black cloak tight to his body to mitigate the snagging and made his way onward.

He had just felt around the poor charred remains of a bear, frowning as burned blood clung to his hands. He wiped the warm viscera on his cloak and peered into the dimness.

Gazlan was not overly worried by the darkness; he could sense his quarry via other means. The necromantic stench overpowered even that of burned flesh, so powerful a magic it was in order to conjure his quarry; its moans and growls grew louder.

It was close.

"You'll be free soon, poor soul. Like these other unfortunate creatures," Gazlan said, his voice muted by the ash fall. He spoke softly, yet he was resolute in his task.

2

He skirted around another poor animal—a moose that was slumped against a fallen log—and reached a shallow ravine in the woods.

His target was down on the ravine floor, thrashing and gnawing at its impossible bonds.

It was a ghoul, its arms suspended from twisted, fire-hardened branches that wrapped around its wrists like shackles. Another tree had collapsed onto it and had wedged its ankle in place. How the ghoul ended up in the ensnaring limbs, Gazlan did not know.

He skidded down the gentle slope, debris riffling in his wake. The ghoul heard his approach and snarled, yanking and thrashing, which caused the branches to twist and snap along with its own limbs. Sinews tore and bones popped out of sockets, but it remained trapped.

Gazlan could climb up to free the poor creature. But the branches would definitely collapse under his added weight. Not to mention he would have to evade the ghoul's reckless attacks at the same time.

No.

He had another idea.

The trees were dead after all.

He steeled himself, biting down the urge to gag, and reached out with his necromancy. Gazlan used the dark arts to feel for the tree that stood strongly rooted into the dead ground. He ignited the foul power with a gasp and brought life back into the stump—or, more accurately, he brought *unlife*.

A green glow permeated from cracks in the tree's charred bark as the ghoul twisted and mangled itself with possessed force. Gazlan gestured, the whole trunk wrenched open. With a rending rupture the tree cracked down the centre, and a red glow lashed out to combat the light of the green necromancy—its insides were still burning.

As the ghoul was freed by the tree's unholy motions, it dropped to the ground, and Gazlan allowed the tree to die again. The green glow and sickly movement died as the orange embers cast a foreboding light about the blackened hellscape.

The ghoul hit the ground with a snap. But a broken spine would not hold back the undead. It shot up, crawling across the ground with a snarl towards the living creature before it. With a sigh, Gazlan strode forward to meet it, catching its arm and reaching out with the foul magics again.

"Be free," Gazlan whispered as he tore the necromancy from the ghoul.

It gasped and sighed, going limp.

Now it was just a corpse, the body of someone who had lived, loved, and struggled. It was someone who had a family and people she loved. It was someone who had been caught up in this pathetic feud against their will and was conscripted to wreak havoc by violence and foul arts.

"I'm so sorry." Gazlan squatted down on his haunches and allowed himself to fall back into the ash, content to let the dying fire warm him until morning.

The choking ash clouds didn't bother him too much; this was not the first place he had seen devastated by fire.

What *did* bother him was movement; the sound of it caught his ear. It was the same kind of monotonous crunch that heralded his own approach through the ash.

He perked up, his head cocking. He could sense no other necromancy nearby, nor any life . . . except for something very bare spreading towards him like the spilling of water, or the marching of ants.

But no, even the critters beneath the ground did not survive the fire.

"Then what is it?" His heart quickened and he sat up, looking up the ravine wall where the sound was coming from.

His heart pounded in his chest as he peered into the dark. The crunching march grew louder, and then a chill ran down his spine as dark, lumbering shapes halted at the top of the slope.

He pushed his awareness further, following the strange trail of life that spilled out behind the shapes. The tendril life intertwined with a snake, *or a vine.* The vine wound itself around something in the form of a person.

"Who goes there?" Gazlan challenged, yelling at the dark shapes, impossible in their presence with such little life force and no necromancy to make up for this fact. "What business do you have with Gazlan?"

"Gazlan?" It was a woman's voice. It was hoarse; she had been weeping and inhaling smoke and ash for days probably. "So that is the name of the necromancer who has defiled my forest?"

"It was not I," Gazlan said.

A smaller figure emerged between the lumbering shapes. Gazlan could sense her fully now, an elf woman; but the life force that spilled from her, into the vine, and then into these lumbering shapes made no sense.

"Then one of your kind did," the elf responded.

Gazlan slumped. "Yes, I'm sorry."

"You will be. Your death comes now at the hands of Vinetta. ATTACK!"

She lifted her hand with a delicate flick, and the lumbering, not-un-dead beasts tore down the slope. As they grew closer in the clouds of disturbed ash, Gazlan's eyes widened. One was the bear he had felt his way around not moments before; one was the moose, and another a bobcat.

But they were dead, and there was no necromancy at play. He could only detect the faint slither of life that was worming its way into these creatures' dead bodies and shudder.

The bear reached the bottom of the ravine first, rearing up to swipe down at Gazlan's lithe form. He expected a growl or a roar; it was more unnerving that the beast was silent. It only gasped as its lungs twitched with vestigial movements.

The necromancer leaped back and rolled over his shoulder as the beast clumsily smashed into the ground. These things were being puppeteered by some magic unknown to Gazlan. He shifted up and leaped away, while the moose charged in from the side, collapsing over the nooks and burned-out husks of dead trees.

The bobcat leaped over the bear as it struggled to pick itself up again and lunged for Gazlan. The beast hit him in the chest and gripped with claws that tore at his cloak and ripped the hood from his face. Gazlan grabbed the bobcat by its forearms and threw it over his shoulder with its own momentum, sending it tumbling into the amber glow of the cracked-open tree trunk. The scant unburned areas of fur on the cat caught fire with a flare of brightness.

In the sudden light, Gazlan took the opportunity to look up at the figure who controlled the creatures, this supposed forest dweller who defiled her own dead.

Her green eyes flared with the glow as the bobcat collapsed limply into a crumpled pile of flames. Her face was contorted in fury, her garments dirtied and dishevelled, and a thick green vine was wrapped around her leg and arm. The vine was teeming with fungi. It wound its way down the slope and embedded into the creatures through their open wounds.

Gazlan had a flash of insight, and then he knew how to win.

Deep down he felt the pull to the easier, more horrid path. He could use his necromancy to ensnare these creatures to his will and sever the strings that Vinetta was using to control their nervous systems.

But he sought the harder path, the path that let him sleep at night.

He reached down into the scorched earth with his necromancy and felt past the dead bodies of critters and insects to find the roots which were charred and suffocated in the acrid soil. He ignited the foul magics once more, forcing unholy life into the dead plant matter as the bear and moose readied themselves to attack again.

It did not matter that the biomass had not joints to move nor mind to think. Because necromancy was now a perverted art. Once a sacred duty, it was bastardised by a man long ago too afraid to face the death of his love, and this perversion was taken on by those after him too afraid to face the living. These *necromancers* imposed a law onto the necromantic arts that none under its influence could disobey.

"Protect your master," Gazlan hissed.

When the bear and moose charged, the dead roots and shrubbery burst from the ground. They formed a mass of twisting, sinewy matter lit within by a green glow and slammed into the mighty creatures with a titanic clash. The moose was impaled onto a branch, which lifted itself into the air—snapping the puppeteer's vine clean from it—and it went limp.

The great conglomerate mass of dead plants and roots reared up as the bear swiped uselessly at it with its claws. The undead biomass slammed down into its spine, filling the forest with the sickening sound of a wet crack.

As the bear twitched, Gazlan knew the vine within it was spreading. It was bypassing the break in the bone and allowing the fungi to seep into the nervous system, commanding it to spasm once more into the fray.

He had to take out the elf.

While his undead forest fought the dead bear, he charged up the hill.

Realising the danger, the elf leaped down to meet him. She whipped a vine with her other arm, and it cracked across Gazlan's face. He fell back with a cry of pain, blood streaking down his cheek. He recovered in time to realise the vine was wrapping around his legs, arms, and neck. Tendrils of fungus were inching closer to his fresh wound.

"No!" He reached down with his necromancy again and brought unlife to all the roots within the hillside.

They burst forth on his command and struck at Vinetta's knees and shoulders, bringing her down as they wrapped and constricted her wrists.

The vine was severed from both of her arms, and the bear's strings were cut. The entrapping greenery around Gazlan's body went limp, and he struggled out of it.

She was still struggling, still reaching out for another vestige of life to manipulate and fight back with. So Gazlan surged up the hill and struck her in the face, knocking her out cold.

The grey light of dawn was fighting valiantly—yet futilely—against the ash canopy by the time Vinetta woke. She was lashed against the burned-out husk of a tree. Undead limbs pulsing with necromancy constricted her legs and bound her arms in front of her, where Gazlan could see them clearly.

She realised that her wounds were cleaned and bandaged, and so she looked to her captor with confusion. He had started a small fire, using the vines she attacked him with the night before, and had a small, bubbling cauldron set over it.

"Your druidry is fascinating," he said without looking up from the cauldron. "Using plant and fungi to hijack the nervous systems of the dead denizens of these woods. Genius, really. You are quite resourceful for a low-tier druid."

"You could have turned my beasts against me," she croaked. "Why didn't you?"

"Because I once vowed never to bind a living soul in agony to its dead flesh. That is actually why I am here." He gestured to the ghoul laid out by the bear, moose, and bobcat. "I have been following the necromancer feud for a few years now, eliminating the aggressors and freeing the enslaved souls."

"So you really *are* different." Vinetta slumped in her bonds as she realised the implications. "I'm sorry for attacking you."

Gazlan caressed the bandage over his cheek. His skin was dark yet pale from his time in the shadows—which reminded him he had to mend his hood. His skin creased under his eyes in heavy bags; otherwise, it was baby smooth. The morning light irritated his flesh, but there was enough smoke cover for now until he could hide his face properly again.

He looked at her and shrugged. "I'm used to it."

"I'm different too." She slumped further. "What kind of a druid defiles the bodies of the creatures of her domain? You should kill me now. No one would miss me."

"You're an outcast too then." Gazlan smiled. "Your skin is rosy pink . . . You are an elf from across the mountains?"

"I was banished when I failed to protect my woods from the undead. Now I have failed again. Just kill me."

Gazlan crushed some herbs and stirred them into his cauldron. "You know, my parents were outcasts too. My mother was a necromancer, my father a druid. People could not fathom the joining of those two wells of power." He sighed. "But the bond they shared seemed nice." He looked at her.

She recoiled in her bonds. "Don't even think about it!"

He rose suddenly—so sudden she flinched—and he waved his hand. The necromancy died from the roots that bound her, and she found herself free.

"If I made you worry in any way by my words, I am deeply sorry. I only bound you to stop you from attacking me . . . I . . . I haven't had a conversation this long with someone in a while. They usually just threaten or attack me." He grinned.

She nervously smiled back, caressing her wrists. "No, it's . . . Let's do this over." She stood and offered her hand. "I am Vinetta of the elves of the rainforests. My Druid Order was of The Vines."

Gazlan considered her hand, then shook it. "I am Gazlan."

She cocked her head. "Is that it?"

"That's it." He released her hand and made to leave as he gestured to the cauldron. "This salve should ease the bruise on your face."

"Where are you going?"

"Like I said, I am on a quest. I will end The War of the Damned and free the ensnared souls that fight it." He stopped, turning. "What will you do?"

"I should tend to these woods, see them grow again." She gazed blankly at the destruction.

"You will die of hunger before this forest regenerates enough to support you," Gazlan said.

"It is what I deserve."

"Doubtful. Just be safe, Vinetta. It has been a while since I had a friendly conversation."

She bit her cheek, considering for a moment. "Here." She tossed him a pouch from her belt.

He caught the bag and examined it. As he hefted it in his hands, the contents rattled against each other. "What is this?"

"Rose seeds." She looked down bashfully. "They're an apology, I guess. They're from my home woods. I meant to plant them here one day . . . I . . ."

Gazlan pocketed the bag of seeds. "I will cherish them. And one day, they will bloom."

He turned from her again and trudged into the smouldering wasteland. Vinetta watched him go, considering her options as she applied the salve to her face and wrists. Finally she trudged after him—at a distance.

Part II: The Swamp of Tears

Long after the fires burned out, long after it would have been of any use, it poured. In the deluge, ash and soil dislodged from the crisped woods and ran into the marshes, flooding them with acrid mud. Once the flooding damage had been wrought, the skies cleared and all was still.

The marshes turned into a bloated swamp.

Insects of plight swarmed the basin, feeding on the expunged corpse of the forest and its denizens in the wake of The War of the Damned. Gazlan paid no heed to the pestilence. Carrion feeders broke far from his path as he drifted towards his goal.

As night fell, a ghastly fog rolled over the swamp, with pale light oozing through the thick canopy to cast a sickly white glow. The muddied waters became an obsidian mirror for the moonlit fog, and ghostly pale light shone over the desolation from above and below, like some terrible dream.

Gazlan glided unnaturally across the flooded plains. The waters behind him only rippled from the passage of his black necromancer's robes as they dragged in his wake. The foul stench of necromancy was on the air. His nose wrinkled, and he cursed his ilk who forsook their sacred duties over death.

The stench was mixed with something else, something sweet from a ways behind him. Vinetta had been tailing him for days now. He smiled, realising he would have to teach her how to properly sneak around if she was to accompany him.

But first, back to the business of the night, he thought.

He paused at a muddy mound protruding from the water; it held a single crushed marshwort. The yellow flower was broken and beaten into the mud by the passing paw prints of ghouls.

He knelt down and plucked the desiccated marshwort from the mound and sighed, caressing the petals. "I'm sorry, my little friend."

He froze as a sound cut through the fog like an ice shard to the heart. It was wailing.

This was a haunted wail, but not from that of the undead, not from the ghouls he sought to free. This was a wail from a living soul.

"It seems you were not the only victim this night," he said, carrying the marshwort in his hands and drifting into the murky fog once more.

After a time he found the source of the agony. The bereaved creature was a man, slumped over the fallen body of his comrade amidst a smattering of dead ghouls.

Impressive, Gazlan thought.

Ghouls were more powerful than the living—the living had inhibitions in order to preserve the body. The dead, not so much, which made them so dangerous. It meant they could strike with the full force of the muscles without paying heed to their own torn ligaments and broken bones. They could suffer more than any creature was capable of suffering and still drag themselves along mechanically to tear you limb from limb.

The young traveller sensed his presence and fumbled through the shallow waters for a large axe. He gripped it with quivering hands.

"Calm, young friend," Gazlan said, raising his hands in peace. "Calm, I am no enemy of the living."

"You are a necromancer?" the man with bloodshot eyes said.

"I'm one of the good ones."

This did not seem to convince him, yet he was too weary to fight and sagged into the waters once more.

"You did well to survive such an attack," Gazlan said.

"He did most of the work." The man gestured to his fallen comrade. "I never could swing a weapon."

"Muscular degeneration," Gazlan said to himself, taking note of the entropic figure of the traveller before him.

"That's what the physicians call it."

"But you shot some of these creatures down?" Gazlan said, pulling a bolt from one of the ghouls.

"He made this for me." The traveller hefted a bulky-looking crossbow from the waters. "Scattershot, he called it. The bolts splinter and multiply as they leave the slide. He made it so I could defend myself if he wasn't around . . ." He choked back a sob. "If he was . . ." He slumped again.

Gazlan crouched over one of the slaughtered ghouls. It twitched and rasped; the soul was still trapped in the horrid form until its master released it. Necromancers never really cared to do that once their servants were incapacitated, and it sent a flush of heat down Gazlan's spine.

He placed his hand on the ghoul's head and murmured an incantation. The body shuddered and the ghoul rasped its last breath with a wisp of green, the soul finally allowed to enter the afterlife. Gazlan rose and made his way around the battleground, releasing the damned from their servitude.

"What is your name?" Gazlan asked between incantations.

"Merigol," he replied.

"What was his?"

"Sinan."

"Who was he?"

"He was mine…" Merigol scrunched his eyes in an attempt to hold back the deluge, "…and I was his."

"I am so very sorry, Merigol." Gazlan released the last ghoul from its curse.

"You," Merigol perked up, looking straight at Gazlan, "you're a necromancer?"

Gazlan paused and sighed. "I cannot do what you hope."

"But I've seen what necromancers can do." Merigol gestured to the surrounding ghouls. "Please, he was all I had!"

Gazlan rose from the last ghoul and stood before the weeping Merigol, still hunched over his love. So much hope in his eyes, so much pain. This would have to be handled delicately.

"He would return a perversion of your love, like these poor wretches who slew him," Gazlan said.

The hope drained from Merigol's eyes, and the deluge resumed as he sobbed over his dead lover.

Delicately, Gazlan chastised himself. "Look, Merigol." He crouched before Merigol and raised his chin to look into his eyes.

"What?"

Gazlan raised up the broken marshwort he had gathered and held it between them.

"If Sinan were this poor flower," Gazlan began, closing his eyes…

He concentrated for a moment, incanting the holy magics that made his profession possible. The yellow flower reconstituted in full bloom. Only it was wicked. The scent turned foul, and vile green pus oozed from the broken, glowing skin of the stem as it held itself together.

". . . He lived, and bloomed, and was taken before his time, yes. But to undo that would be to undo him, his life and impact. This flower provided beauty, some bee pollinated it, took pollen from it, it provided sustenance for creatures in this plain, supported the soil it grew in . . . and then its life was cut short. To restore it artificially would be to usurp what it had worked for, to destroy the delicate world that it was a part of.

"Your Sinan left his mark on the world. He changed you, altered the trajectory of your life. If you were to prop up his corpse, your life would become venom, like the venom leaking from this flower."

Gazlan released the magic, and the flower sagged and died again. He produced a seed from his satchel, crushed it in his palm with the dead flower, and plunged it into the waters. He drove it through the acrid top layer and into the earth beneath the surface, chanting again.

An entirely different magic swirled beneath the waters.

Not his magic—not all of it—Vinetta lent her aid from the foggy veil.

"But if you were to use the experiences his life gave you," Gazlan continued. "Let it fuel you. Let it direct your life that you have now, then you yourself can bloom into something different. This is not a betrayal. It is helping him stay alive through his memory, through his legacy. Here." He pulled his hand from the watery earth and held a rose, red, thorned, and perfect. Moisture glistening in the pale foggy moonlight clung to the petals like encrusted jewels. "I became a necromancer to protect that process..." He paused. "To honour the ones who I have loved and lost... It will take time."

He offered the rose to Merigol, who took it with trembling hands.

"It won't be easy. I do not envy the journey you have before you. But the gift of Sinan's life can keep on giving, if you let it." He rose. "Or you can stay here... and become the corrupted marshwort."

Merigol gripped the rose close to his chest and bent over the form of his dead lover once more. "Just go," he sobbed. "Leave me be."

"I leave you then, with all the love I can muster," Gazlan said. "And I am sorry for what has been taken from you."

"Just... leave."

"If you can manage it, you can join me on my quest. I am pursuing the necromancer who commanded these ghouls. You could find justice. But I understand if you decide to stay," Gazlan said before turning from Merigol.

Gazlan breathed in the rich, damp air and scented more perversion of life in the distance. He glided into the night to pursue it.

Merigol did not react when Vinetta emerged—clumsily—from the fog. "Come, Merigol. It is not safe here, and Sinan would not want you to grieve alone."

Merigol eyed her wearily. "A necromancer and an elf find me in the depths of hell and offer to lead me out. Perhaps I should take that as a sign?" He grabbed his crossbow from the waters. "But I can't leave him here."

Vinetta wove her hands, and the magic of druidism swirled between them. "Say your final goodbye, Merigol. I will ensure that the earth keeps him safe."

Merigol started as the roots deep below the surface rose through the dead soil and foul waters. They gently embraced Sinan's body. Fumbling, Merigol took a locket from his lover's neck and watched as he was pulled reverently below the waters to rest within the earth.

"Goodbye."

Part III: The Paladin Tinkerer

The mishmash party left the marshes some days ago, only travelling during the night—much to the chagrin of the two stragglers who tailed the necromancer at a distance.

Now they were close to the great grass plains—the acrid stench of the marshes was nothing but a foul memory, and the pestilent swarms grew thin.

The sun was setting over the golden prairie as Gazlan readied to set out again, and gentle wisps of wind caressed the long grasses. Gazlan halted on the brink of a rolling hill, scanning the vista as he waited for his distant companions to ready themselves.

He knew Vinetta was following him.

And Vinetta knew that *he* knew she was following him . . .

He took a moment to process that thought.

He wondered why she would not just travel openly with him. He then realised she probably felt awkward about trying to murder him with marionette beasts. He would feel awful too were their places reversed. But Merigol . . . he was unsure why Merigol lagged behind with her. Perhaps he was still trying to reconcile that he was now on a quest with a necromancer, when it had been a necromancer who caused the demise of his lover.

Gazlan shrugged.

It would be harder for them to pretend to sneak in his wake over this terrain. It was only a matter of time before they became proper travel companions, and he wasn't entirely sure he was comfortable with that. He had been alone this whole time, after all.

These thoughts were pushed from his mind when he noticed a problem on the horizon. As the golden disc of the sun dipped below the world, he caught a glimpse of a shimmering image that faded into the amber sky. It reeked of danger, and something in his bones made him want to recoil and weep at its presence. But he also felt that another necromancer was close by, not a day's journey past the direction of the fleeting mirage.

He steeled himself and set out into the darkening prairie. At least he felt safer at night.

And at least he was not *really* alone.

Night fell quickly, and the dry grass crunched underfoot in the dark. It was stirred by a dry, cold breeze that made his sweat sting as it slid down his brow like ice. He stopped to wipe it away before it seeped into his eyes. This was not normal. His eyes darted from one dark expanse to the next; there was no hiding place for the source of his dread.

"Who goes there?" His voice belied the panic that rose in his throat. "What business do you have with Gazlan?"

"Gazlan?" The hollow darkness echoed his call, gruff and palpable.

Something gripped at his heart, tangible fear. The world of the dead was bread and butter to a necromancer, but a formless voice that belonged to the corporeal? That was something he did not understand.

"Who goes there?" Gazlan repeated, his voice rising.

There was a blinding flash of white light, bright like the sun but a thousandfold more dazzling upon the field. Gazlan hissed and recoiled at the touch of it and crumpled to the ground.

"Paladins!" he cried, understanding now his sense of dread. "I am not your quarry!"

And what's worse, perhaps a dozen paladins to cast a light so bright.

He retreated as far under his robe as was possible, crouched and cowering like a roach when he heard them. Their limbs creaked as they marched in tandem from the source of sheer light and encircled him. And then there was one that was different than the rest, one with the lumbering gait of someone huge.

The thundering footsteps halted before his quivering form and growled.

"Not so tough without your ghouls." The voice reverberated within Gazlan's bones, deep and powerful. It shook with rage. "Come out into the light. Allow yourself some redemption before the end."

"My redemption will come with another's end!" Gazlan whimpered. "I am not your enemy. Please, the light."

The paladin reached down with his weapon, and the blade of a mighty battle axe slid under Gazlan's hood and touched his chin. Against his will, his head was tilted upright, and his skin was exposed to the great light that hovered motionlessly above them. The silhouette of his captor towered over him, an outline of broad shoulders, pointed ears, and a wide jaw. It was an orc . . . an orc paladin.

Gazlan bit his tongue as he summoned his unholy powers and reached into the soil. The light burned his innards while the two antithetical forces raged against one another. Paladin magic was a conduit for Holy Sun Fire, and the light burned all necromancers as a curse for their kind's sins.

The orc paladin laughed. "Your shadow cannot blot my fire."

"No," Gazlan squirmed, "but the earth can."

He reached for the dead matter along the topsoil. No dead deep roots and trees to appropriate this time. Instead he found the dust between the grass and the decaying matter of each blade that wilted for another to take its place. He breathed the foul un-life of necromancy into the barest patch that he could manage. His captor sensed Gazlan's inner battle and cried out, pulling back his axe to strike an executing blow.

But he was too late.

Gazlan flexed his necromancy, and the dust and decaying matter pulsed with green and shot into a ball between them. With the holy light nullifying his powers, he had to concentrate on each molecule. Gazlan could not rely on the defending laws of necromancy to take over and aid him. So he flexed his jaw, and the ball of dead, pulsating matter shot up to smother the light, clobbering the paladin on the chin along the way.

Something crystalline cracked, and the light fractured into wavering beams.

The green glow of necromancy writhed and pulsated with hellish reds and warpish violets as the balls of darkness and light fought their own war.

With the light nullified enough and the orc recoiling, Gazlan shot up onto his feet and struck the closest paladin with a blow to the face. The bones in his hand cracked upon impact with a hard wooden surface. He recoiled, gripping his hand and screaming a confused profanity as his foe tumbled back lifelessly.

Ignoring the pain he rounded on the next paladin to see it standing motionless in the flickering dark.

"What the hell is going on?" Gazlan screamed. "Who are you, Paladin?"

The orc got his footing and roared, spreading his arms. The light above them died, as did Gazlan's ball of dead matter when his concentration was broken by the battle cry. The orc shot beams of light—weak, pitiful excuses of paladism—towards his inert, wooden companions. The light struck them at key crystalline points, illuminating them briefly before they began to jolt and spasm back to life.

"Machines, they are robotic machines?" Gazlan breathed in disbelief.

"And they will be your end," the orc said.

"Why do you need them to fight for you if you have an army of paladins? You would have to have had dozens of companions to have created an artificial sun like that."

"That was another creation of mine," the orc grunted. "It was a bulb which trapped and amplified my light. Just for show really." He shrugged, stepping back.

Gazlan readied himself as the light-powered, mechanical warriors raised their weapons to attack. He clenched his uninjured fist, struggling to logic his way out of the impossible situation.

"Gazlan, down!" The cry came from the darkness.

Gazlan hit the ground as Merigol emerged with his modified crossbow and pulled the trigger. The specialised bolt rang as it left the slide, splintering into a fanning flurry of barbs. Gazlan tensed. He was still within the cone of death.

In the same instant a rumbling came from below, and a living root—deeper than anything he could sense—erupted from the ground. It created a barrier between him and the errant bolts that impacted into it. Several hit the mechanical warriors. One copped it to the chest plate, and it flailed in a shower of splinters and sparking sunlight; another was struck across the leg, and it spun to the ground. A third got smacked in a glowing eyepiece, which shattered, and the light powering the thing flitted out. The warrior went limp but remained upright.

"Who defends the blight bringer?" the orc bellowed.

"I am Vinetta of the Rainforest Elves." Vinetta emerged from the dark next to Merigol. "And this is Merigol of Frenk. You attack a friend of the living. As a druid, I must intervene."

"This necromancer?" The orc pointed his axe at Gazlan on the ground. "A friend of the living?"

"He released the ghouls that killed my husband," Merigol sputtered. He was fidgeting with his crossbow, trying to pull back the slide, his dark, sweat-soaked hair plastered to his forehead. "He hunts the necromancer that conjured them."

"I keep trying to tell you!" Gazlan cried as the remaining mechanical warriors regrouped, forming around the orc and himself. "I am not your enemy!"

"I have heard tales of a Nunnadan-born necromancer who can also bewitch the mind," the orc said. "You may have done the same to these two people."

"Only a select few Nunnadan have the ability to perform that magic," Gazlan growled. "It requires the right bloodline and many decades of training. I am not yet thirty. I am a necromancer of the old ways. I seek to end the plight that my fellow class are enacting on these lands. Please, let me pass."

"Do you know what the last necromancer who came through these parts did?" the orc roared. "She sputtered and begged for aid, claiming to do battle with the Nunnadan I speak of *in the name of the old ways.* We let her into our monastery, and she poisoned everyone! I have spent the last weeks seeking and freeing my brothers and sisters from their curse. I only survived because I was so engrossed in my work, I did not hear the bell to come feed. I was spared in my solitude."

"Allow me to aid you." Gazlan extended his hand. "I can sense their corpses on the plains. Without your paladism to cloud my necromancy, I can feel them. They are surging towards us, towards the source of conflict between your power and mine. Let us put your order to rest so that their souls may enter the sun and continue to give life to the world."

The orc growled low within his chest. One of his mechanical men raised its own crossbow at Merigol as he finally managed to reload his. Vinetta whipped a vine from her belt, and it curled around her arm, ready to attack.

"How many of your people remain?" Gazlan asked. "Please, they will be upon us soon, and my quest does not end with their salvation."

"There are seven more of my order to bury. If they rush us en masse as you claim, my paladism is not strong enough to fight them off. It was never strong to begin with. I relied on my strength and my wits when paladism failed me. I can't win, not with my light post destroyed, not with my cogs damaged as they are."

"You channelled your mediocre power into a formidable force, friend." Merigol stepped forward, tentatively lowering his crossbow. "You put down Gazlan, who Vinetta tells me is no easy foe. You have created these mechanisms to supplement your power and your own warrior prowess. And now you have a necromancer here to aid you, a druid . . . and me, for what good I'll do. We can do this, together."

"Please," Gazlan said, his hand extended and trembling. "Allow me to guard the passage from the world of the living to the afterlife, as my kind should."

The orc grunted and grabbed the hand. He hauled Gazlan to his feet as his cogs lowered their weapons, and Vinetta's vine slinked back around her waist.

"My name is Wutarl the Meek." The orc paused. "My tribe once ousted me for my tinkering, and the paladins kept me downtrodden for my dim light. But now I am all that is left of both of those people."

"Let us help you honour both your people." Gazlan shook the mighty yellow-skinned hand and winced as his cracked bones sent shoots of pain up his arm. But that pain was nothing compared to the presence of more paladism. "You can let down your mirage now; we have work to do."

Wutarl grunted again, turned, and waved his axe. The mirage Gazlan had seen earlier wavered before them in the dark and dissipated, revealing a humble camp with a hastily erected palisade and smouldering fire. There was a chaotic workbench by the tent overflowing with gears and mirrors and the chassis of his cogs.

"Using light to create a mirage." Merigol whistled. "You sure are creative."

"How long do we have?" Vinetta stepped forward, brushing the dust from Gazlan's hood before she pulled it over his head again.

She pulled a small jar from her leafy sash and applied the balm in it to his injured hand. It smelled of crushed rose and soothed his shooting pain. He smiled weakly at her, and she smiled softly back, before turning away.

"I reckon we have some minutes," Gazlan said, flexing his hand as the pain dissolved. "Let's make ready."

The dry breeze turned foul. Merigol gagged upon his roost behind the palisade. The smell was nothing measured against the swamp he was found in, but compared to the clear air of the prairie, it was a punch in the gut.

He eyed Wutarl standing across the makeshift gateway. He had yellow, softly scaled skin—typical of a mature orc—and wore heavy mail over his large bulk with a tattered green and gold tabard. He had donned a pair of cracked half-frame spectacles—hilariously small on his mighty head. He never stopped glaring at the necromancer, not during their scrambled preparation, and not now while they waited in silence.

Gazlan ignored it; he was used to the instant hatred of the living. He often even felt it towards himself.

"The grass is trodden underfoot by blighted feet," Vinetta whispered. Her brow was furrowed as she focused her druidism on the grass by the gateway; her rosy pink skin had turned bright red. "They are close."

She was pressed up against the palisade right by Gazlan, and the hushed tones of her wispy voice sent tingles down his neck. He was unsure if this was a pleasant sensation or not. Maybe it would have been better had she and Merigol kept their distance from him until he figured things out.

"I sense them," Gazlan said, tensing.

"Relax, Gazlan," Vinetta said. "You have survived worse... I attacked you with worse."

Gazlan nodded and relaxed as best he could. Her words did not comfort him; he knew that a pack of ghouls was more dangerous than the puppets she attacked him with. He was just glad she thought he was tense because of the danger and not her proximity.

"Now?" Wutarl growled.

Gazlan sighed. "Now." And he scrunched his eyes shut.

With a roar, Wutarl swung his axe towards the heavens and called on his holy power. The axe glowed briefly with sun fire, and Gazlan's innards revolted against him. Beams of light shot from the blade and shone on the translucent, crystalline plates on certain joints of his cogs. The mechanical warriors whirred as the light reacted with chemicals to power their bodies, and they readied to defend the gateway.

The ghouls screamed and writhed at the presence of paladism. Gazlan bit his lip not to scream with them. Despite their pain they swarmed towards the light-driven robots, urged on by the enslaving power of necromancy. Rushing into the gap at the gate, they quickly overwhelmed the cogs, and Gazlan gave the signal to Vinetta.

With a release of tension, she let go of her druidism. The blades of grass beneath the gateway un-wove from each other, collapsing into a shallow pit as the thin veil gave way and the combatants collapsed into the hole.

Merigol leaped up from his roost above the gateway and fired down into the pit with his scattershot. He struck ghouls and cogs both, pinning many in place amidst the mess of limbs and wood and decayed claws.

A straggling ghoul rushed in the gate and avoided the pit, sprinting for Gazlan. He pushed Vinetta back, and it tackled him to the ground. It was so fast, so powerful, that it knocked the wind from him. He was unable to draw breath to speak his spells. He looked up in horror at the gaping, bloody maw of the poor corpse on top of him. It snarled, revealing rotting flesh intertwined with broken teeth and a mutated tongue lathered in rancid bile, which dripped down onto his skin. The lifeless eyes gazed at him in pain, in fury and despair, and it readied to clamp its dislocated jaw around his head.

It snapped back.

Vinetta's vine whipped it across the face with a violent crack, and its jaw fell clean off onto Gazlan's chest. With a cry of fury it leaped from Gazlan and barrelled after her. She channelled her druidism; shoots of grass sprang up and ensnared the poor thing. It tore from its restraints, ripping flesh and snapping bone as grass shoots were uprooted by its efforts.

Vinetta was backed up against the palisade; it was inching closer through her barrage of vine whips and grass snares. It reached for her with filthy, mutated claws, and she screamed.

Gazlan gasped his first breath of air since being winded and grabbed the ghoul's leg, incanting his spell. With a shudder it went limp, finally dead.

He turned to find a number of ghouls climbing from the pit. Wutarl stood at the lip, striking down at the creatures as they grasped for purchase to climb. Gazlan was grateful the orc was not using his paladism but instead battling with his raw power. He realised that Wutarl's holy power must have been spent... He did mention he was weaker than other paladins.

Merigol had loaded another bolt by now and shot into the writhing pit. A ghoul evaded all shots and leaped out, gripping Wutarl's neck. With a roar he hefted the hapless creature through the palisade in an explosion of splinters and collapsing posts. He charged after it with his axe raised, hewing it into pieces.

The ghouls were rising behind him in his battle rage. Gazlan rushed to his aid, standing at the lip and freeing the ghouls from their corpses as they freed themselves from the pinning bolts and the pit. Vinetta took up position on the other side of the hole, using her vine whip and grass snares to help slow them as Gazlan did his work.

Within a few minutes, the frightful task was done.

Gazlan stood across from Vinetta, panting in silence as Wutarl wailed outside the camp.

"You saved me," Gazlan said.

"You saved me," she replied.

"... Thanks."

Gazlan shuffled from the aftermath and out to Wutarl, who had devolved into sobs. The orc had his hands on a body, trying to chant through his blabbering, trying to summon holy light to free the soul from its torment.

No light came. He was exhausted.

Merigol stood watching on the roost as Gazlan approached Wutarl cautiously. An interaction he had been a part of not nights ago, now looking in from the outside.

Gazlan knelt by Wutarl and released the soul of the masticated corpse. "Are all of your order now accounted for?" he asked softly.

Wutarl nodded. "Her name was Firna," he choked. "She was the first one to welcome me into the Order of the Radiant Star. She stopped the others from teasing me for being a tinkering orc, for being an orc at all, for being a poor paladin."

Gazlan placed his hand on Wutarl's shoulder. "Come, friend, let us bury her."

"What am I going to do now?" Wutarl sobbed. "My tribe was slaughtered by a band of trolls, and now my order has been killed . . . twice."

"You can accompany our strange band," Gazlan said, unsure of himself. He turned back to Vinetta and Merigol, who watched on silently. "That is, if you can stomach to travel with me and not behind?"

"I was just unsure," Vinetta said. "I tried to kill you the first time we met."

Wutarl's sobs were interrupted by a brief laugh.

"It happens." Gazlan shrugged.

"You said you sought the necromancer who did this?" Wutarl asked.

"There are five more feuding bastards behind this," Gazlan answered. "I am after one most of all. But make no mistake, I am after them all."

"Then I will join you."

32

The four worked tirelessly into the night to lay the bodies of the paladins within the pit with dignity. They struck camp and set out as the sun rose, with Gazlan retreating under his robes. The first golden beam of light lashed out across the prairie to caress the soft earth where fresh graves now lay. All that signified the gravesite was a single planted rose, a token from the gift Vinetta had given Gazlan.

Part IV: The Witch Hat Abomination

The mass of diseased arms swayed like grass in the gentle breeze. Gazlan could not see their faces, only the rolling plains of limbs as lost souls cried out for salvation.

Could he give it to them?

A crack of lightning splintered the darkness, and the turbulent sky surged against itself in a churning maelstrom. Green necromancy pulsed and swirled around the eye of the storm, and another bright light struck down from the abyss, searing the field of limbs with a sickening, sizzling stench.

"Gazlan!" The voice rose over the deafening cries. "Come!"

Gazlan started awake with a scream. But calm soon returned. The burning light in his dream was only the first rays of sun as the dawn crept gently over the plains.

"You were having a nightmare," Wutarl grunted.

The orc was tinkering with Merigol's bow, adding gears and mechanical switches. He glanced briefly at Gazlan over his comically undersized spectacles. Gazlan wiped the sweat from his face and pulled his hood down to protect him from the light, and from the scrutiny.

"Where are the others?" Gazlan rasped. His dread and panic subsided as he found peace in the cool dark of his robes. "Where is Vinetta?"

Wutarl raised an eyebrow.

Gazlan slinked further back into his robes.

"Merigol and Vinetta decided to head over to that ridge. See what they could see." Wutarl's deep voice reverberated within Gazlan's skull.

"Merigol made it up the ridge?" Gazlan asked.

"I used the chassis of one of my cogs to create an exoskeleton for his legs. He should find it easier to travel at our pace now."

"Good," Gazlan said, rising. "Good. He needs an easier time given what he's been through."

The silence stretched between them as the sun rose. The light—as harsh as it was to a necromancer—soothed the terror of Gazlan's dream. Darkness tainted many thoughts; the light was a necessary burden to bear at the moment. As he stretched out the stiffness from the night, Gazlan breathed deep . . . He sensed another necromancer was close; he could smell the stench of their power.

Soon.

"Why him?" Wutarl's gruff voice broke his concentration.

"What?"

"Why did you bring Merigol with you? The elf I can understand . . . well, now I understand . . ." Gazlan looked away as Wutarl chuckled. "But a fellow human, one with weaker limbs. Why?"

"It was that or leave him to fester in a putrefied marsh. I already had Vinetta tailing me. It seemed . . . better, to have someone with her," Gazlan answered.

"Ah," Wutarl huffed. "You're afraid."

"Of what?"

"Of getting close to the elf. You wanted a buffer to help bridge the gap between you and her."

Gazlan felt his cheeks flush hot. "I wouldn't put someone's life in jeopardy for such a reason! Yes, I am afraid, of travelling with people again. The last time I ran with another, I watched him torn apart! But I couldn't just leave a man to grieve in those waters. I couldn't! How dare you suggest otherwise?"

Wutarl stood and towered over him. Gazlan's voice dwindled to a squeak, but he still glared up at the orc in defiance.

"I just wanted to grind your gears, so to speak, to test your motivations." He removed his spectacles. "I am afraid too. I have already lost so much. I wanted to see if you would lead these people to ruin in pursuit of pointless gain."

"I might," Gazlan said, "but they would have died if they remained where they were."

"Hmm, I still don't trust you, Necromancer. But I think your intentions might be pure."

"I guess we'll see."

"Your elf friend returns. Merigol is coming too." Wutarl smirked.

Gazlan glared again before greeting Vinetta and Merigol.

"Nice legs, Merigol," Gazlan remarked.

"Thank you!" Merigol beamed, gesturing to his legs and hopping on the spot. "Wutarl whipped them up. I barely even limp now!" The wooden exoskeleton ran down his legs and encircled his boots and waist. "I just need Wutarl to power the ... cells?" Wutarl nodded. "Every so often."

"The sun itself can power them," Wutarl added. "So avoid late night walks in dangerous territory without me around."

"Yessir!" Merigol saluted smartly.

"So what did you see?" Gazlan asked.

"The prairie is dying over the ridge," Vinetta said quietly.

"Blight," Wutarl growled, "I can sense it."

"Me too," Gazlan sighed.

"There is a ruined town in the distance; it looks as if it has already fallen. There are a lot of vultures circling overhead," Merigol said. "Do you think it would be safe to move through there?"

"Are there any other towns nearby?" Gazlan asked.

"There is a river that runs from the north." Wutarl pointed northwards where the ground steadily rose. "It was where my monastery was located. The necromancer who destroyed it is probably making her way down the river, on the way to the coast, where I hear one of her rivals has been raising an army. There is only one other town close by, about a week's march on foot, that's if she is on foot."

"Then the necromancer is still at the town you saw," Gazlan confirmed.

"How do you know?" Vinetta asked.

"Because I can sense her ghouls. She would keep the bulk of her army nearby in case of reprisals from the living on her way towards her enemy. Are we ready for a fight?"

"Is this the necromancer whose ghouls attacked Sinan and me?" Merigol asked.

"It is most likely," Gazlan said.

"Then I am ready."

"I will die trying to slay this witch," Wutarl said, smashing his fists together.

Gazlan eyed Vinetta.

"Whether it was her who burned my forest or not, she must be stopped," she said.

"Then let's check out this ridge," Gazlan said.

The four stood atop the rocky outcropping with the creeping dead land beyond. The grasses withered into dust and blight even before their eyes. There were barren outcroppings of stone and sparse trees as the prairie gave way to the river land. Half-tilled farms and untended roads littered the expanse. On the distance by the rolling river was a town. It was ramshackle, teetering to collapse into the river to be slowly carried out to sea. There were a few smouldering fires within that expelled wisps of foul smoke into vulture-infested air.

"Where are they?" Merigol asked, fidgeting with his crossbow.

"In the basements," Gazlan answered, "or the crypt, the silos, or the barns. Ghouls and sunlight don't mix. It reminds their flesh that the soul should be on its journey towards the great light. It burns them."

"Why don't you enjoy the sunlight?" Merigol said suspiciously.

"Because necromancy fell into the hands of the evil and malcontent. Necromancers have forsaken their role in the natural world. They used to journey from one damned place to the next, freeing wraiths and spirits that were trapped before they could pass on." Gazlan sighed.

"Then some maniacal fiend used that power to trap souls within the bodies, to make slaves for themselves," Wutarl growled. "The Sun Guardians—protectors of the afterlife—charged the paladins with expunging that evil, granted the power of holy sunlight to help us combat them. Until balance is restored, no necromancer will walk easily during the day."

"Even the good ones?" Vinetta asked.

"It keeps me focused," Gazlan said.

"How long has this struggle gone on?" Merigol asked.

"Some thousands of years," Wutarl said.

"The War of the Damned is a recent feud," Gazlan said. "Some of the necromancers fancied themselves powerful enough to be lords over the living *and* the dead. The silver lining is that it has gone a long way to scouring most of the evil practitioners. Though, it's done so at the expense of the living. Come. We have work to do."

The mismatched party descended the ridge and made their way over the blighted plains towards the town.

"If they are in the crypt," Merigol asked as they walked, "wouldn't they be able to summon the hundreds of people buried there?"

"No," Wutarl said, "only those whose souls are still close by. If they have made it to the afterlife, their souls are safe and shine down on us every day." He gestured to the sun. "But we will likely face many hundreds of ghouls regardless. The town alone would have swelled her ranks."

"How can we prevail?" Merigol asked.

"We fight off the ghouls until we can forge a path to this necromancer," Gazlan said. "I am powerful enough to force her to heel."

"And then I will kill her," Wutarl roared.

Gazlan halted. "I am not here to add to the dead."

Wutarl turned back to face him. "Neither were my paladins."

"Well, this is new. A necromancer wanting to preserve life while a paladin seeks to kill?" Vinetta said. "Let's not get at each other's throats yet, boys. We could decide on a course of action and plan it to perfection, but knowing our luck, it would fly right out the window the moment the ghouls rushed us."

"Your girlfriend has a point," Wutarl said.

Vinetta's rosy ears turned bright red.

"She's not my girlfriend!" Gazlan stammered. "But yeah, she's right. There is no point in planning what we'll do with this necromancer *after* we've defeated her. We'll very likely be fighting for our lives." Gazlan continued on, surging past Wutarl and Vinetta.

They marched on in silence. It took the better part of the day to reach the town, and even their quick rest stop was cut short by the foul stench that rose from the dying earth. The sun was entering the cusp of twilight as they cautiously strode through the unhinged gates.

It was almost quiet.

The houses groaned as the weather cooled, hanging signs squeaked on their chains in the breeze, and there was the unnerving sound of rasping and shuffling just on the edge of hearing. Evidence of the town's sacking was rife across the streets with litter and broken windows and doors. Then there was the blood that dripped from the surfaces and stained the street.

No bodies though.

The party slowly made their way into the town centre. It was a three-way junction as the main road ricocheted from the crossing, heading out the other end of town. The other road headed towards the river, where a mill turned gently. The corners of the junction held the sheriff's office, the tavern, and the butcher.

"The three signs of a healthy society," Merigol muttered as Vinetta scrunched her nose at the meat shop. "Meat, booze, and a place to sleep it all off afterwards."

"Four." Gazlan nodded down the main road.

The others followed his gaze. The road ran by the town temple, elevated on a mound of hallowed earth with a slanted door leading underground—the crypt.

"That seems like a good place to host a mass of clumsy bodies," Vinetta said. "We have the river hemming us in down that way . . . We are too exposed here in the centre."

"We would be exposed outside the town walls as well," Wutarl grunted as he un-shouldered his pack and rummaged around. "Better to get it over with."

"Did you see that?" Merigol trained his crossbow on the tavern; green light flickered between the slats of the wall.

"That's a temple of light." Gazlan was still looking at the temple and ignored Merigol. "I doubt the necromancer would set up shop in there. The ghouls are likely spread out throughout these buildings. They have been watching us since we arrived."

A cackling laugh sounded from behind them, above the sheriff's office. They rounded on it as something on the roof scurried away out of sight.

"That was her," Wutarl snarled. He produced a collapsible wooden post and began to set it up.

"She's a fast one," Vinetta said.

"She's a gnome," Wutarl said. "I nearly got her back at the monastery, but she scurried into all of the hard-to-reach places until she could raise enough ghouls to drive me away."

"Well," Merigol said, scanning the rooftops with sweeping motions from his crossbow, "damn."

"She will be damned soon enough," Wutarl replied. "The lamp post is ready; it should provide us a safe haven from the ghouls . . . for a time."

"Light it up." Gazlan was watching the skies shift from scarlet to deep shades of night. "The world grows dark."

As the sun dipped below the horizon, the tavern door burst open, and a band of ghouls screamed out of it in a mass of thrashing limbs. Wutarl chanted with his hand on the post. It flared to life and created a circle of warm light around the party, a bastion against the dark. The ghouls screeched and skittered to a halt on the edge of the light, and as true darkness settled over the lands, more of their kind poured out of their dark hiding places to rush the centre.

The party looked out to a mass of moaning corpses that shambled over one another to attack them, only to shrink back at the light. Wisps of green necromancy sparkled in their eyes, and the budding moonlight shone off exposed bone, meaty textures, and gnashing teeth . . .

"Some hundreds," Gazlan said. "What was I thinking?"

"What were you thinking indeed?" A shrill voice rang out over the din, and the ghouls went silent.

The party looked back to the sheriff's office as a pointed witch hat scurried out to the lip. Merigol whipped around his crossbow but hesitated.

"What?" Merigol said.

"It's just a witch hat?" Vinetta said.

The shrill cackle returned, and the hat jostled with it, tilting back just enough for the party to see the tiny gnome who was balancing it on her head.

"Ginnalor!" Wutarl cried. "I will crush your puny skull!"

"Now, now, Orc!" The gnome laughed as the hat slipped down over most of her body. She used her tiny hands to lift it back up. "Would your order appreciate you making a comment so hurtful to my people? Perhaps we should ask one of them?"

"I released each member of my order, Witch!"

"And he had help." Gazlan stepped forward.

Ginnalor started, before laughing again. "Oh my, a young necromancer thinks he can stand up to me! At last I can give up my petty disputes and bow down to the King of the Damned!" Her shrill laughter was echoed by her ghouls. "I will add you to my ranks, amateur!"

"Ginnalor the Red, is that right?" Gazlan said calmly.

She halted and the witch hat tilted towards him. He had her attention.

"I have heard of what you did to your own people. I have felt your necromancy from afar for weeks now. I know that you have defeated several other contenders in your pathetic feud before I could intervene. I have with me a druid who looked after the forest that burned as you slew Ragjar the Tall. I have a traveller who lost his world when you marched over the trade route to Frenk. You already know my friend Wutarl the Meek. You have grown overconfident. In me and my companions, you will find only humiliation and defeat. Unless you release these souls now in the name of the old ways and answer for your crimes, you will die here in this town."

Ginnalor was silent for a moment, looking hard at Gazlan before inclining her head with a smirk. "Oh, so if I don't surrender to have my skull crushed by that brutish pretend paladin . . . I'll die?" She winked. "Young Nunnadan. You have no idea the feats I am capable of. You have no idea the enemies I have been preparing to face."

"I do."

"You are nothing," Ginnalor continued, "but soon your lives will have purpose; soon you will all serve me!" The witch hat spun, and a dagger was flung from it to smack into the bulb on the light post.

The paladism was snuffed out with a shattering, and the ghouls surged inwards now that the light had died.

"You've made your choice," Gazlan said as the light left his face.

He was chanting before the first ghoul hit him. Upon contact it fell to the ground, inert. Behind him Merigol shot his scatter bolt, and the fanning destruction cut a swathe into the first rank of ghouls. They stumbled over one another as he pulled back the cocking mechanism Wutarl had installed, and a new bolt slid effortlessly into place for him to shoot immediately.

According to Wutarl he had about ten shots before he had to reload a magazine of bolts. Each shot slowed down the next wave as the ghouls had to scramble over the incapacitated who were struggling to rise.

Wutarl held back the next quadrant. With a roar he threw a cluster of objects onto the ground and lit them with paladism. The ghouls shrieked as the tiny, scattering bulbs burned them with holy light. With enormous swings of his axe, he cut down the ones that were unfortunate enough to make it through the field of light.

Vinetta held back the remaining side. With a cry in elvish, she threw her hands towards the sky and summoned the vultures who had been circling for days. In a frenzied swarm they swooped down like a wave and pushed the ghouls back. Pecking at eyes and disorienting the creatures as they stumbled and tripped over one another.

While the vultures gave her space to breathe, she unfurled the vines from her waist and whipped out with them. She buried the vines into the undead corpses, and the tendrils of fungi and mosses that clung to her weapons seeped into the nerves of the dead to create a force of marionettes to protect her.

Their nervous systems struggled against the pulsating necromancy that compelled them to kill in the name of their master. But it created a dozen or so meat shields for her to use for cover as she struck out with her vines and her vultures struck from the skies.

Gazlan was climbing over the growing mound of inert corpses as he continued to chant and siphon the souls from the damned bodies to the afterlife. The mound was growing large enough that he was rising above the battle and was but a short leap from the sheriff's office's roof. As Ginnalor commanded more ghouls to swarm towards him in her desperation, he was able to add more to the mound of the dead, getting closer to her.

"No!" she cried, shuffling back when Gazlan climbed over the gutter and onto the roof.

The witch hat spun, and another knife flew out to embed in his flesh. Gazlan weaved out of the knife's path and drop-kicked the gnome, who even with the tall, pointed hat was barely as high as his knee.

They sailed away—gnome and witch hat both—to the other side of the roof, and Gazlan surged after her to press his advantage.

A ghoul's fist broke through the ceiling from below, and the ghoul clambered up to stand between Gazlan and his target. In the battle below, the desperate group found that as they were about to become overwhelmed, the ghouls broke off and swarmed up the corpse mound to protect their master.

Gazlan glanced around as the ghouls rose over the edge.

"I have bodies to spare, Nunnadan," Ginnalor spat, righting herself and pulling her large hat in place. "What have you got in place of an army, a band of misfits? You have no thralls to aid you! Necromancer indeed."

"This atrocity you call an army is not true death, Witch Hat." Gazlan knelt and reached out with his power. "True death is selfless; it is balance. It is matter giving way and feeding more matter. It is the soul—enriched by its lived experience—travelling to the afterlife to live in paradise as it shines that life force back on the plane of the living. What you have here is a perversion." He channelled his necromancy into the river, into the soil and blighted earth, searching, finding, binding. "A weakness." He grunted as he ignited his power. "I will show you the true power of death!"

A flash of green tore down the river and across the fields. The blighted soil shifted and churned. Gazlan had found all of the dead matter—microscopic motes of dust, bugs, and plant stuff that had withered and which the blight had multiplied tenfold—and he massed it together beyond the village wall.

Ginnalor scrambled onto the shoulder of one of her ghouls to look out and see the pulsing ball of blight and necromancy. "How?"

"This is true power. And I didn't have to enslave anything to wield it," Gazlan said through gritted teeth.

He smashed his fist into the roof, and the blight surged forth like a dust storm over the town. It slammed into the mass of ghouls above and below, sweeping them away and parting around Gazlan and his companions.

Ginnalor was knocked down onto the roof by the hurricane with a squeak as her ghouls were blown away in the gale and stripped to shreds by the microscopic particles. And then, as if nothing had happened, the blight storm ceased. The town was scoured smooth by the sands and reflected the silver moon. The ghouls were nowhere to be seen, shredded and scattered in organic tatters.

Gazlan placed his boot on the sprawled Ginnalor and pressed her into the roof with increasing pressure. "Those poor souls are still in agony. Release them."

Even as she squeaked under his weight, she cackled, "Not a bad trick, young one. I think I know now where I recognised you from."

"It doesn't matter."

"Oh, but it does. Did *he* really think he could send another to strike me down in his place?"

"He is next on my list, don't you worry." Gazlan pressed harder. "Now release them!"

"What was that?" Vinetta pulled herself up onto the roof with her vine as Wutarl assisted Merigol in climbing up.

"It was a lesson," Ginnalor squeaked. "I may not be able to control that much dead matter on my own, young necromancer. But you just created building blocks for me, all powered by their own souls."

"What are you playing at?" Gazlan barked.

"So perhaps I can do something similar with those poor shredded ghouls . . . but with a bit more pizazz!" She bit Gazlan's ankle.

Gazlan swore and recoiled. Ginnalor took her chance, breaking free and scurrying away as Wutarl charged in to smite her. When his axe struck the roof, she scurried into the hole her ghoul had made for her.

"I didn't like the sound of that," Merigol said, reloading his scatter bow.

"What did she mean?" Wutarl asked, his nostrils flaring in rage. "What is she going to do?"

"Shit." Gazlan felt a pulse of necromancy.

"Shit?" Vinetta asked.

A green pulse flashed throughout the town, cumulating wherever there was shredded ghoul.

"Shit!" Gazlan cried. "Get ready!"

The shreds of ghouls began to shift and churn just like his mass of blight did. The fleshy chunks pooled into the three way intersection and massed, forming the shape of a man. And then it continued to mass, and mass, and mass. The dead matter rose over the sheriff's office to tower over the town as a giant formed from the churning shreds of corpses.

"This is an abomination!" Wutarl struck out with a weak beam of light and it seared a pitifully small gash in the abomination's side.

Ginnalor's cackle rang out from the creature as the gash widened to reveal her nestled within, channelling her necromancy to keep the horror together in green pulses. "Once I have defeated your friendly necromancer, I will try to keep you all alive long enough to suffer before you finally serve my will!" The wound in the abomination closed, and the giant mass lifted its arm to strike at the roof.

"Get down!" Gazlan cried.

The party scrambled over the edge and fell to the road as the sheriff's office was obliterated by the abomination's strike. Debris rained down around them while Wutarl leaped up and helped get his winded companions to their feet.

"Keep moving!" He turned to summon more paladism to strike back.

"No!" Gazlan gasped. "Save your power. I have a plan."

A shadow loomed over them as a great foot attempted to smush them into the dirt. The party sprinted across the street and into the tavern, and the roof exploded into shards of wood. The abomination reached in to grab them, but they were already scurrying out the other side.

"Oh, is this what it feels like to tower over others? No wonder we gnomes are downtrodden!" Ginnalor cackled. She struck out indiscriminately across the town, and the party struggled to stay ahead of the destruction.

"So what's your plan?" Vinetta yelled as they ducked through an alley and sped towards the mill.

"I have enough strength left to channel a blight storm strong enough to fling one of you up there!" Gazlan gestured to the abomination that was bearing down on them.

"What good would that do, Necromancer?" Wutarl growled as they scurried into the wider road.

"Merigol," Gazlan said, "get your bow ready. Wutarl, as soon as he shoots at the abdomen, you channel everything you've got into the wound. Vinetta, you'll need to cut in with your vines."

"You're flinging me?" Vinetta squeaked.

"Do you trust me?" He shot her a look over his shoulder as they ran.

"I guess I owe you for raising an army of beasts against you," she panted.

They reached the end of the road at the water mill and turned to face off with the abomination bounding towards them.

"Debt is not trust," Gazlan said. "I'll try to change that if we survive this. Wutarl!"

Wutarl raised his axe into the air and roared. The axe blade pulsed with weak light but steadily grew brighter. The earth shook when the abomination stepped closer, and Ginnalor's cackling reverberated within it.

"Merigol!"

Merigol aimed for the thing's gut and pulled the trigger. The scatter bolt ripped a large swathe, and the churning mass of ghoul shreds rippled. With a mighty bellow Wutarl flung his axe, which tore towards the closing wound and cut a searing path further into the abomination.

Gazlan had been summoning what dead matter he could to the mill wheel. It spun wildly as it pulsed with necromancy and teetered on its axis, flinging the waters everywhere. He eyed Vinetta, who had her two vines spiralling around to a point above her head.

She nodded.

Gazlan cried with exertion and channelled the blight which had been spinning around the mill into another storm. It picked Vinetta from the ground at speed and flung her into the now closing wound that Merigol and Wutarl had created in the gut of the abomination. She oriented herself so the spiralling point of her vines became like a drill head and slammed into the wound as it closed over. A split second later, she burst through the other side with Ginnalor in her arms.

The two spiralled to the ground, and Gazlan used the last of his strength to summon a cushion of blight in the air to slow their fall before impact. Vinetta drove her shoulder into the gnome, slamming her into the ground with what little force remained in their fall.

Ginnalor squeaked as the air was knocked from her and the witch hat tumbled away. The abomination stumbled and fell into tatters. Wutarl was already charging with a battle cry through the descending cloud of ghoul with his secondary axe. Vinetta rolled out of the way as he leaped through the air and cleaved the gnome in two.

There was a gasp when the souls were released from the masticated shreds and the green pulse of necromancy ceased.

Gazlan was panting, his vision white as he tried to stand amongst the snowing bits of corpse. Merigol rushed in to assist him.

"I tried to give her a choice," Gazlan panted. "I know you think she did not deserve one."

"I know." Merigol gripped him tightly. "But we freed these people from their hell. We avenged Sinan and Wutarl's order. You did good, Gazlan."

"Vinetta?"

Merigol smirked. "She is safe. Rest now, Gazlan. Rest."

Gazlan sighed and let unconsciousness take him.

He awoke sometime later to the scent of Vinetta's crushed rose salve all around him. He peeled his eyes open. His three companions sat around a fire in the town centre, all bandaged and looking as beaten as he felt.

"So we did survive," Gazlan said.

Vinetta turned and smiled as he struggled to sit up. "Stay down, you took quite a beating."

"We all did," he protested, but he allowed her to press him back down again.

He watched her while she checked over his wounds.

"What are you looking at?" she asked, a small hint of blush appearing at the points of her rosy, elven ears.

"You trusted me." He grinned. "No one has done that in a while."

She smiled, looking away. "Yeah, I guess I did."

"And I guess I trust you too, Necromancer." Wutarl's gruff voice cut over the crackling fire. "But I'll still keep you at an arm's length."

"That's quite far . . . for an orc," Merigol said, elbowing Wutarl.

"Heh," Wutarl grunted, "we can't make it too easy on him, can we?"

Gazlan tuned them out as they continued their beautiful, inane banter, focusing on Vinetta, who applied more salve to his wounds. "Perhaps we should plant one of those rose seeds here. Mark our path on our quest," Gazlan said.

"And why is that?" she asked.

"They are a gift I greatly cherish. I want to share that gift. Plus," he eyed Merigol, who bore his rose on his lapel, "they seem to be our thing now."

She reached into his pouch and produced one of the seeds. "You know," she said, considering the seed carefully, "that isn't such a bad idea."

Part V: The "A" Team

"Just come on out, Gazlan!" Merigol said.

"No!"

"Gazlan," Vinetta said sternly, "come out this second so we can see how it looks."

"No!" Gazlan repeated.

Wutarl growled a laugh. "Heh, the necromancer is like a frightened rabbit."

"Shh!" Vinetta menaced Wutarl with her vine and then subsided. She turned back to the tree Gazlan was hiding behind with a smile. "Gazlan," she said sweetly. "We don't want anyone in town to suspect you're a necromancer and try to lynch you. We won't laugh; Merigol did a fine job sewing the decorations on. Just come out and we can go in, get some information, and have a decent meal for once."

The three waited as Gazlan sighed, "You better not laugh."

"On my honour," Wutarl growled.

"Okay." Gazlan took a deep breath.

He stepped slowly into the firelight. Floral designs—from flowers summoned by Vinetta—were stitched into his robes. They crowned Gazlan's dark hood like a reef, danced around his sleeves to encircle his cuffs, and formed trimmings along his buttons down to the hem.

Vinetta smirked, Merigol nodded in pride at his work even as his lips curled into a smile, and Wutarl . . . Wutarl burst out laughing.

"Hey, you promised!" Gazlan's skin flushed, and he slinked back behind the tree as Vinetta and Merigol joined in the laughter.

"It looked so good, though!" Vinetta teased. She raced around the tree and dragged Gazlan back out. "Ignore the orc! You certainly don't look like a necromancer anymore. Just try not to walk as if you're gliding when we head into town." She examined the designs up close. "The colour is quite striking against the black. Good job Merigol."

Merigol didn't answer. He and Wutarl were supporting each other as they collapsed into a deeper fit of laughter. Gazlan stood self-consciously while Vinetta fussed with the robe.

"Your face when Wutarl laughed!" Merigol was in tears.

"He looks *cute*!" Wutarl roared, gripping his belly. "The necromancer looks *proper* cute!"

"I hate all of you!" Gazlan stamped his foot.

The party had moved beyond the rolling prairie and travelled down the river for some days now, entering the hilly woods that buffered the river land from the coast. After more days of bushwhacking and eating the slim offerings the overly scavenged woods had to offer, they found themselves camped on a ridge on the outskirts of a town.

Now with Gazlan's disguise, they could enter freely . . .

. . . Mostly freely.

It was late afternoon by the time they reached the heavily guarded gates in the palisade. They were greeted by a gruff-looking sergeant who was backed by a squadron of spearmen and covered by keen crossbowmen on the lookout towers.

"I need to check you all for a pulse," the sergeant said, wearily eying the travellers.

After a brief examination, the sergeant relaxed and waved the party through. The crossbowmen lowered their weapons and called the guards on the inside to open the gates.

"If you're continuing along the same direction you've been travelling," the sergeant called to them as they shuffled through the gates, "try to die *before* you lead the dead back to this town, yeah? If you're still alive at the head of a swarm of ghouls, we'll shoot you down."

"We will not be the ones dying," Wutarl growled.

The sergeant chortled at that. "I've heard that before."

As the party entered the town proper, they attracted strange looks from the disquieted locals. Gazlan was worried they were looking at him, but it was mostly Merigol's exoskeleton legs that drew attention. The attention was short-lived, thankfully; stranger things had evidently happened in these parts as the folk carried on about their days without comment.

It was a mostly human town, with two-storey wooden buildings and thatched roofs, simple and vulnerable.

"This place is heavily guarded," Wutarl said, "and oddly, not guarded enough. They could not hope to have repelled the force that Ginnalor was about to bring to bear on them."

"I think they knew that," Merigol said, sauntering over to a noticeboard along the main road.

There were serious-looking decrees and notices warning of the undead hordes converging on their location. With one expected from the river some days ago.

"I guess we put a stop to that," Vinetta said.

Gazlan squinted at the map of ghoul sightings. "But *they* don't know that. Why wouldn't more of the army be here to defend it?"

"They're defending the shipwright on the coast," Wutarl grunted, gesturing to the map.

"Stupid bastards," Gazlan cursed. The map showed the shipwright had a small town nearby which was bolstered by the army's presence, but the majority of villages along the coast were mostly left to their own defences. "The necromancer on the coast wouldn't give a damn about the shipwright. Or if he did, he would simply attack it once he'd enslaved the souls of the poor undefended townsfolk."

"Perhaps they were pushing the necromancer up towards the sea?" Vinetta traced the path of a larger force that was apparently pursuing the coastal necromancer's movements.

"That force could hinder the necromancer, yes," Gazlan said. "But his concern was Ginnalor the Red, which was probably why he was massing to meet her ... here, I guess. But he would have sensed the absence of her power and concluded she was slain. His next move would be to go after the next rival in the War of the Damned."

"Who is?" Wutarl asked.

"I know there is a chain of islands across the strait which is under strife," Merigol said.

"The Dwarf Islands?" Wutarl asked.

"I hate dwarves," Vinetta spat. "Always trying to make me eat mutton. They don't accept that I'm fine without meat. It's such a foreign concept to them, they think you'll starve and so they try to force-feed you."

"Their compassion sounds disgusting." Gazlan elbowed her.

"Don't you get started, flower boy!" She laughed as her barb set him tense again.

"So if this coastal necromancer is heading across the sea, he will attack the shipwright?" Merigol asked.

"No," Gazlan said, "he wouldn't want to get caught between two armies without another necromancer to help divide their attention. He'll head for the nearest sea town and enslave as many souls as he can along the way."

"A coastal village won't have the transport he needs to ferry an army across to the islands." Merigol spoke as if perplexed.

"An undead army doesn't have the same needs as a living one," Gazlan said. "Okay, we rest and resupply here for the night and head out first thing."

"Finally, a decent meal for once!" Wutarl bellowed to the skies.

The townspeople started at his outburst but quickly recovered and scurried about their business.

"I don't recall you cooking once since we linked up," Gazlan said.

"Don't get so testy, *flower boy*!" Wutarl mimicked Vinetta's tone.

Gazlan tensed again as Wutarl and Merigol laughed, heading for the tavern.

"You really could have cooked one night, though," Merigol said to Wutarl as they left.

"Come on, Gazlan, you look great." Vinetta pranced on after them.

Gazlan grumbled curses to himself as he unclenched his fists and followed.

"I think your clothes are lovely, mister!" A little girl with bobbing pigtails bounded alongside him.

Gazlan stopped and considered the girl. He was unaccustomed to a lack of fear from the living, and this was strange.

"Why thank you, young one," he said. "I will try not to let the gilded orc get under my skin."

The girl smiled as Gazlan entered the tavern after them. Unbeknownst to him, the girl turned to the hooded figure waiting down the next alley and nodded vigorously before skipping away.

The hooded figure removed a rolled-up decree from his cloak and ran his finger down the calligraphy.

Wanted, it read.

For the crimes of Necromancy in the War of the Damned.

Ginnalor the Red – Gnome of Dusty Peak, pale skin, hair of red copper.

Ragjar the Tall – Human of Dwet, pale skin, hair of black . . . tall.

Junla Roosewat – Drow, unknown origin, dark blue skin, black pointed hair.

Sscrell – Naga of Trine, described as a sea monster.

Towards the bottom of the list, the hooded figure stopped.

Ubzlan the Terror – Human of Nunnadan, dark skin, short black hair.

The figure nodded. "How many Nunnadans do you suppose wander this land?" he said.

"I'd reckon just one, this near the coast," a woman's voice rasped from the shadows.

The first figure chuckled, circling his finger around the last line on the decree.

Reward for proof of death – 10,000 Cets each.

"Looks like we have a chance to take him down before the army does. Inform the team, we have a payday looming."

The four travellers sat around the table, bantering blissfully as they ate. Wutarl and Merigol feasted on roasted lamb legs, Vinetta had a bowl of greens, and Gazlan a humble porridge.

"You see," Merigol said, "my Sinan was a tinkerer too." He slurred his words with the levities of the night. "I just think it's nice to see he was in good company."

"He sounds a fine man!" Wutarl boomed. "For a human! Hah!"

The patrons around the tavern booed at him in mirth. No matter the barbs, it seemed good for their morale to have a paladin in their midst, one who was also a mighty-looking orc.

"Too right!" Merigol cried. "Boo the orc; look at how small his spectacles are!"

This prompted a laugh, and Wutarl growled in mock anger.

"Perhaps a song would ease the cultural tension? My order taught me the paladistic chants, and I composed a mix with them and my tribe's war songs!" The patrons cheered Wutarl on.

Wutarl stood—stumbling slightly—and cleared his throat.

His singing was hoarse and guttural, but there was a harmony that resonated within it as tribal chants blended with holy hymns. It was a strange synergy between two worlds that had the patrons laughing initially, but they quickly silenced in keen interest.

"It is actually quite lovely, isn't it?" Vinetta said, sidling up to Gazlan.

"Mmm." He sipped from his mug. "Wutarl continually surprises me."

"I guess we all have that in common." She rested her head on his shoulder as she quietened to listen.

Gazlan felt his whole body go rigid, but he pushed the feeling to one side. His heart was hammering, which rattled his breath but also sent warm, soothing shoots through his chest. In an attempt to distract himself from this and the fact he felt he could not breathe, he reached into his pouch of rose seeds and held one before Vinetta.

"You have something on your mind?" she said in his ear.

"These are more than just a keepsake from your home woods, aren't they?"

"They were from my family's garden. We elves do not die frequently. But when we do, we bury our ancestors in the rose garden. These seeds are a part of them; the essence of the first druids flow through them even to this day. When the ghouls overran the woods, I was charged with defending the rose garden. I failed. These were all I could save. I was exiled, charged to find a safe haven for their essence to persevere in order to redeem myself. That place burned down before I had the chance."

"And you gave them to me?"

"You..." She paused. "Planting them is more of a metaphor ... It's hard to explain. But I felt drawn to you, and I trusted my instincts. Now these roses grow from Frenk to the coast. One rests on the lapel of a worthy man." She gestured to Merigol. "One grows to mark the site where a town of souls was saved, another over the graves of once-loved paladins. Maybe that's what my ancestors wish to do now? Stand watch over the forgotten and the meek who have struggled for life despite the horrors of the world."

"That seems profound and confusing," Gazlan said.

"I'm drunk." She giggled. "But I was drawn to you. Tell me about your father."

"What?" Gazlan tensed.

"The Druid."

"Oh. Well, he found me on my own really."

"Didn't you say he fathered you with a necromancer?"

"Well," Gazlan sighed, "my mother didn't spend long with him. She was taken, right before me ... He was crippled and found me wailing in a ditch ..."

"I'm so sorry." She caressed his cheek.

Gazlan savoured the sensation before continuing. "So he raised me on his own, taught me of the original nature of necromancers like Mother wanted. As my power grew, so did the enemies I attracted. More necromancers came, and we fought them off, until one day we didn't. He was taken from me too, and I embarked on my quest."

"It seems we have all experienced pain," Vinetta said.

"There will be more, before the end," Gazlan replied.

Wutarl finished his song, and the patrons cheered.

"Come, we should get some rest. We have an early start tomorrow," Gazlan said.

The party set out just before dawn—like they always did to ease Gazlan's journey. They headed out of town and further into the woods, which grew rife with ridges and outcroppings of rock as it sloped higher. Once they reached the peak of these slopes, they would be able to see the ocean and perhaps sight their next target.

Gazlan could sense him. He could sense his massing army of the dead. And he could sense the fury bubbling within himself.

Soon.

Vinetta stopped in her tracks. "There is something strange afoot."

"What do you mean?" Wutarl asked, sniffing and scanning the sloped forest.

"The birds have gone silent. I haven't seen a critter since just after dawn." She unfurled the vines around her sash.

At her preparation, Merigol cocked his crossbow, and Wutarl pulled the axe from his back; the grating sound when the haft slid across his chain mail set them on edge. Gazlan clenched and unclenched his fists as he reached out with his necromancy.

"I sense nothing," he said, "other than our next foe on the coast some days away."

"In a war-torn land the living can be just as dangerous as the dead," Merigol whispered.

The four stood at the ready as the trees bristled in the breeze.

Waiting...

Nothing...

"Hmph," Wutarl growled. "Perhaps, Vinetta, it's that you just can't handle your grog?"

She shot him a look, but Gazlan raised his hand. "Shh."

He heard something, the crack of a twig, the sliding of fabric over the brush. He cocked his head—ignoring the shaft of sunlight that peeked through the canopy to stab at his face—and stepped forward to hear better.

Then there was a louder snap.

A snare tightened around his leg and went taut as a log fell from a tree across the way. With a yelp Gazlan was yanked off his feet and suspended upside down.

"Bandits!" Merigol shot his scatter bow into the brush. A single arrow whistled from the canopy and sliced the twine of his crossbow in response. "Curses!"

"Taste the sun!" Wutarl bellowed as he summoned a beam of paladism from his fist and aimed it towards the arrow's origin.

There was the sizzling of leaves and a boisterous laugh. A large man in plate armour burst through the brush with a war hammer and returned his own beam of light. It caught Wutarl in the chain mail, refracting off the blessed armour as a rainbow, and the force of the blow knocked him off his feet. Gazlan cried out and shielded his eyes.

The newcomer laughed. "What a pathetic paladin!"

"You bastard!" Vinetta surged forward with her vines to attack.

With a boyish grin the paladin blocked one vine with his hammer and allowed the other to whip uselessly at his breastplate. Then a hooded figure shifted from the underbrush and clobbered Vinetta's knee with a cudgel. She swore and faltered to the ground as the rogue slid a knife over her throat.

"Stay still, hon," she hissed in Vinetta's ear. "Wouldn't want to cut ya."

The archer swung from the canopy on a rope and alighted before Merigol. Merigol struck out with his disabled crossbow. The archer caught the feeble blow with one arm and pulled the weapon from Merigol's entropic grip.

"Valiant, if futile." The archer struck Merigol across the face and knocked him down, discarding the crossbow in the same motion.

"Who the hell are you?" Gazlan spat. "Why the hell are you attacking us? We don't have coin for you to pilfer, you bandits!"

The archer cocked his head and removed his hood, looking at Gazlan's upended face sideways. He was middle-aged with grizzled stubble and a scarred face.

"Is this him?" the archer said, grabbing Gazlan's hood and pulling it back.

A goblin hobbled out of the brush with a looking glass strapped to one eye. He hopped up onto the archer's shoulder and examined Gazlan's face closely.

"Dark skin, poorly disguised black robe, aversion to paladism . . . probably why the orc struck out so weakly. I'd say it's Ubzlan the Terror, for sure," the goblin hissed.

"That orc tried his best. Sadly *his best* was not better than mine," the enemy paladin boasted with an arrogant laugh.

"Ubzlan is as old as this goblin looks!" Gazlan snarled. "I am too young to be him."

"How many other Nunnadan necromancers are there?" the rogue holding Vinetta captive asked. "How many Nunnadans period? Didn't you wipe them all out when you started this war, Ubzlan?"

"There are a select few who still stand against him," Gazlan said through his teeth. "I am not the man you seek."

"Well, I don't believe him," the goblin said.

"Even if you did, the bounty office would likely still pay us for his head," the archer replied.

"Worse than bandits," Vinetta said. "Bounty hunters."

It started to grow dark.

The paladin tutted. "That's a derogatory word! We are simply a party of humble adventurers."

"Worse than bounty hunters, Vinetta," Gazlan said, growing woozy as the blood rushed to his head. "Self-proclaimed heroes."

"Self-proclaimed?" The archer leant on his bow to scrutinise Gazlan. "We are doing the fine work that our fellow military cannot. Taking out the enemy where many others have failed." He gestured to Gazlan. "Case in point. We're the A Team, baby!"

Gazlan laughed.

"You find that funny?"

"I do." Gazlan laughed harder.

"This one is crazy," the goblin said.

"They all are . . . but I wanna know what's so funny." The archer struck Gazlan across the face.

Vinetta swore and struggled under the rogue's grip.

"Just kill him, Bluken," the rogue said through her scarf.

"I wanna know what's so funny!" Bluken struck Gazlan again.

"The A Team?" Gazlan coughed. His head was swimming, but he just needed a moment longer to concentrate. "Any party of *heroes* who could describe themselves as the A Team have either swelled the necromancer's ranks already or are actually defending the innocent, as heroes are wont to do. Anyone else is a military stooge or an absolute moron. You lot are the D Team at best."

"Yeah? And what kind of team would you call this then, huh?" Bluken pulled out his arming sword—a wickedly curved scimitar with blue runes—and held it up to Gazlan's eyes.

"We're . . . the Rose Squad," Gazlan said.

Now the goblin and the paladin laughed.

"Well, the Rose Squad got beat pretty easily. We just took down the greatest necromancer in this war without so much as a fight. As if we aren't the A Team!" the paladin said.

"The real A Team would have noticed how dark it was getting." Gazlan chuckled. The bounty hunters looked around, realising that it was a shade darker than normal. "They would be asking questions, listening for what could cause such a thing. They would be looking up the rope they tied the necromancer to, wondering why it is starting to pulse and wriggle . . ." He waited as they looked up the rope, now looking away from Vinetta, who was chanting under her breath ". . . and they would wonder why an orc with enchanted armour would go down without so much as a death rattle."

"Where is the orc?" Bluken asked hurriedly.

"Why, he fell into the brush over there." The paladin pointed with a stupid expression spreading across his face.

"Make sure he's down," the goblin barked. "Stupid jock."

A brutish war cry sounded from the brush. "Prepare yourself, Gazlan!"

A contraption flitted into the ambush, a device with whirring wooden blades that kept it afloat.

Gazlan scrunched his eyes shut and pulled his hood over his head.

The device flashed with a blinding light, and all except for the antagonistic paladin cried out in pain as they shielded their eyes. Vinetta head-butted the rogue who held her and shot her arms free. She commanded the torrent of leaves and critters that she had spent the last moments gathering to the tree canopy to swoop down and attack.

Gazlan bucked and wove his necromancy into the dead fibres of the rope that bound him. It pulsed with green light and snapped free from the chaotic branches above, striking at Bluken and the goblin. It whipped them together and bound them as the squirrels and leaves surged for the paladin.

The rogue recovered and slashed Vinetta's side with her knife. Vinetta stumbled into the brush, and the leaves fell softly as the critters fled in panic. While the enemy paladin was surging out of the foliage in a daze, Wutarl screamed into the fray. He clobbered the rogue with the butt of his axe and knocked her out cold, then charged the paladin who had grabbed his war hammer in the chaos.

The titanic clash of axe on plate and hammer on chain mail rang throughout the churning woods.

While the paladins did battle, Gazlan ensured that his rope had successfully bound Bluken and the goblin. Wutarl was struck repeatedly by a rapid combo from the enemy paladin, who finished it off with a light blast that knocked the orc back through the undergrowth.

Gazlan reacted quickly and summoned his necromancy. He pulled the dead matter around him to shoot it out like a lance. But he was not quick enough. The paladin turned to face him with an outstretched hand and fired a beam of light.

The light shot through Gazlan like a spear, and he fell back with a pained cry.

Merigol had been restringing his crossbow in the confusion and rose as Gazlan fell, shooting the scatter bolt. The fanning cone of death struck and ricocheted off the paladin's armour. But several bolts found the chinks, embedding in shoulder joints and glancing off the paladin's brow.

The paladin swore as he dropped his hammer and fell to the ground with blood in his eye. He was writhing in pain, disabled.

"Anyone else?" Merigol scanned the forest, re-racking another bolt into his bow.

Wutarl and Vinetta pulled themselves from the ground, readying to support Merigol if their enemies still had fight in them.

The rogue was out, Bluken and the goblin were bound, and the paladin tried uselessly to pick up his hammer with his injured shoulder joints. After a moment he gave up, falling back into the undergrowth with another swear.

"Didn't think so," Merigol said, swinging his crossbow up onto his shoulder.

"Gazlan!" Vinetta rushed to Gazlan, who was writhing on the ground.

A hole was burned through his chest; the wound was partially cauterised by the searing light, which was the only reason he still lived.

"It passed through his heart!" Wutarl said.

"No, it only grazed it." Vinetta inspected the wound in a panic as Gazlan moaned. "His lung also got seared, and the beam burst right through his other side. He hasn't got long."

"What can we do?" Merigol asked.

"He is holding on by a thread. I don't see how we can save him unless we can repair his organs. My salve can only do so much. Wutarl, can your light heal him?" Vinetta looked up desperately.

"Even if my healing light was strong enough, it would only harm a necromancer more."

"Shit!" Vinetta's eyes danced over Gazlan, stopping at one of the roses embroidered into his hood. "I have an idea, but it might not work, and it might kill him."

"It is a better chance than he has now," Wutarl said as Vinetta rummaged through Gazlan's pouches.

His hand reached out and gripped onto hers. "Vinetta," he rasped.

"Shh, Gazlan, shh," she cooed. "Just breathe as best you can."

She found the pouch with her rose seeds and produced one. She placed it within Gazlan's wound and then smeared her salve over the entry and exit wounds. He groaned and she gently hushed him again, caressing his face.

"What are you doing?" Merigol peered down in curious horror.

She placed her hand over the wound and began to chant in elvish, spinning her druidry into the seed. A snapping echoed dully as the seed churned, and Gazlan writhed in pain.

"You're killing him," Wutarl said.

"Wutarl," she gasped. "I'm not strong enough to grow it how I need. The rose, it needs light."

"It would kill him faster," Wutarl said.

"Just a faint glimmer! Please! If he survives your light long enough, my power will heal him. I just need a little boost!"

Wutarl growled, "Fine, but it is not going to be pleasant. Merigol, hold him down as best you can."

Merigol crouched by Gazlan's head and held down his shoulders while Wutarl wiped away the salve from the wound and inserted his finger.

Gazlan cried out and bucked, nearly throwing Merigol from him.

"I'm ready," Vinetta said.

Wutarl grumbled and channelled light from his fingertip into the half-germinated seed in Gazlan's chest. Vinetta gasped as she found the life force she needed to make this work. Gazlan screamed and writhed, and Wutarl had to use his free hand to help press him down into the ground. Shoots of necromancy pulsed from his body, stirring the dead forest matter like a dark wave.

"That's it, Wutarl, get out of there!" Vinetta ordered.

Wutarl pulled the bloodied finger back to see the green of the rose stem weaving itself into tendon and muscle, the thorns curve and intertwine to shape into bone, and the petals encase the scorched heart and lung.

The petals pulsed with his heartbeat and the swell of his haggard lung as the wound healed layer by layer. Finally, Vinetta's salve mended what flesh it could on the surface. Gazlan's writhing turned to convulsions and frothing at the mouth before he finally went still with a horrifying death rattle.

Vinetta gasped as she released her power and grabbed at his face.

"Give him some air," Merigol said, waving her back.

Gazlan lay peering up into the tree canopy, which was spackled with sunlight. He did not wince or recoil from it.

"Is he . . . ?" Merigol asked.

"No!" Vinetta sobbed. "No, not now, not just as we were . . ."

Gazlan sputtered and coughed, rising with a terrible cry.

"By the Sun Guardians, it worked!" Wutarl boomed.

"What in the damnation just happened?" Gazlan breathed. He was gripping his chest. "I feel . . ." he breathed deep, ". . . fresh?"

Vinetta laughed and threw her arms around his neck. "We had to make some alterations to your heart as well as your robe . . . so people knew you weren't a terror."

Gazlan stared wide-eyed for a moment before laughing, himself, and returning her embrace.

"Thank you," he said, "all of you." His skin had gone pale, but colour was starting to return to his face.

"Now what of them?" Merigol asked.

The four companions stood over the A Team. They bound the rogue and paladin to Bluken and the goblin as they gathered their things and disarmed them. Gazlan took the scimitar from Bluken.

"I might need something extra where we're going." He flourished it briefly before tying the scabbard to his belt and sheathing it. "Beautiful markings. These are mage runes, yes? Good for severing a bound soul from a ghoul in a pinch."

"Are you going to kill us?" the paladin asked.

"We should," Wutarl growled, menacing him with the war hammer he had taken. He had the paladin's plate armour strapped tightly over his chain mail. The plate looked as if it had shrunk as he wore it; it was designed for a human after all.

"We will leave you tied up here. The village trappers have some snares set up nearby. I'm sure they'll find you lot eventually," Vinetta said with her hands on her hips, by the rogue's knife and cudgel strapped to her waist by her vines.

"So long, D Team." Merigol saluted and laughed. He twisted the looking glass strapped to his eye—a gift from the goblin—and the glass expanded and retracted as he fiddled around with it.

The four turned from the bound bandits and made up the slope.

"So you aren't one of the bad ones?" Bluken called after them. "You're really going to try to stop this mess?"

"I'll stop the mess caused by the damned. And I'll go through any of the living who try to stop me!" Gazlan replied over his shoulder.

"We should really be more vigilant in future," Wutarl said, slinging the hammer over his shoulder with his axe.

"True," Merigol answered. "And if we get into close quarters again, I might need an exoskeleton for my arms . . . Wutarl?"

"Aye, I can do that." Wutarl halted to unpack some contraption from his travel sack to tinker with while they marched.

Merigol waited for him as Gazlan and Vinetta pushed onwards.

"The Rose Squad, eh?" she said, nudging him with her shoulder.

"Fitting even before your . . . alteration?" He clasped his hand around hers. "You saved my life again."

"Hmm, don't get used to it," she teased.

Gazlan smiled, but his mirth wore off easily. Ubzlan the Terror. It was almost certain now that he was the necromancer harvesting the living along the coast.

He was close, and Gazlan could feel his power growing.

This next battle was going to be hard. He'd known it would come to this ever since he set out on this quest. But as they halted for Wutarl and Merigol to catch up, he felt some small hope.

Maybe, he thought. Maybe with this motley band that was becoming a family they might actually prevail. He felt at the flowers on his hood, felt the rose that beat with his heart and swelled with his breath, felt the warmth of Vinetta's fingers between his, and allowed himself to smile.

Part VI: The Terror of Nunnadan

The Rose Squad stood upon a wooded ridge that granted them a grand view of the horrifying vista as it tumbled down into the gentle stretch of land before the beaches. They watched, helpless, as the constant wailing drifted on the winds to their vantage point. The coast was in chaos; the scattered communities that dotted the shoreline were aflame or smouldering as an army of shambling terrors crept into the largest village.

Its people fought a tenacious and desperate last stand. But ultimately they were overwhelmed, and Ubzlan the Terror set his forces—bolstered by his new victims—swarming into the sea.

On a different day, the coast would have been quaint, pleasant even. The white sands lined the immense bay that the destroyed communities called home, and the waters were a calm black in the setting, smoke-veiled sun.

"Does he expect them to swim?" Wutarl asked. His heavy voice was now no more than a whisper.

"If he did, he would not mass them at the jetties," Vinetta said.

"We'll know more once your device returns." Gazlan bit down, forcing back the rising bile in his throat.

He could sense them all, the dead and decaying masses. It was like in his dreams, a maelstrom of the damned. The voice of his enemy's necromancy taunted him, and the thousands of souls screamed in a language only he could understand.

They cried out for salvation.

Could he give it to them?

A whirring interrupted his thoughts.

Merigol raised his arm, sporting a brand-new exoskeleton that Wutarl had constructed to aid his muscular degeneration. A device drifted into their camp and nestled into a socket by his shoulder—another of Wutarl's contraptions.

The orc had used his paladism to channel sunlight into a power cell he'd tinkered together, which powered the device's propellers to give it flight. It was the same device that had triggered the flash bomb when they were ambushed by the *A Team*.

He called it a drone.

Wutarl muttered to himself as he detached the drone from Merigol's exoskeleton and removed a cartridge. A light-sensitive plate had been installed beneath it.

"It'll trap the light at a certain time and present an image of what was below it," Wutarl had explained earlier.

He summoned paladism to his finger and shone light over the still image.

Gazlan recoiled briefly at the light, but leaned in with interest at what it revealed.

"So this is what a bird's eye would see?" Vinetta wondered.

"Could you not use druidry to see the same through a bird's eyes?" Gazlan asked.

"There aren't any around; even the vultures have fled or died," she lamented. "I never thought to actually see through their eyes, though . . . That would feel wrong."

"Can we focus please?" Wutarl showed the image, a snapshot of the sea village that had just been overwhelmed.

"Are those whales?" Merigol asked.

"He sent his ghouls into the sea to attack pods of whales," Gazlan said through gritted teeth, "and used them to hunt down more sea beasts, and then more. Now he marches his ghouls into their bloated bellies to transport them across the sea to his next rivals."

"Is there no end to a necromancer's villainy?" Merigol cursed. "Sorry," he said to Gazlan. "Obviously not you."

"No, no, I'm with you," Gazlan said.

"It does provide us with an opportunity," Wutarl said. "We can let him transport the bulk of his army into the depths. There will be less might to defend him when we close in."

"He will travel conventionally on the boats with an honour guard," Gazlan said, circling his finger around the few boats docked in the town. "Some hundred or so ghouls and a selection of grotesques." The others gave him a look. "A grotesque is when several souls and corpses are bound into one flesh, forming a brutish corpse. Not unlike the abomination we faced when fighting Ginnalor, in theory. When those thousands dwindle to hundreds, we will have to strike."

"And so we wait," Vinetta said.

"So we wait," Gazlan confirmed. "Get some rest, if you can."

Merigol and Wutarl settled in for the night as Gazlan looked back out over the dying coast. Vinetta slinked next to him.

"You aren't tired?"

"Curious," she replied. "Do you know this Ubzlan?" Gazlan was silent. "Those bounty hunters said he destroyed your people?"

"I know of him," Gazlan finally said. He turned to her with a pained smile. "My mother and I fled Nunnadan when he harvested it for the first strike in The War of the Damned."

"That must have been so awful," she whispered.

Gazlan took in a breath to speak, and Vinetta looked at him, patient and kind as he hesitated.

He looked back at her a long moment, her eyes filling some deep longing in the depths of his being. They stirred something, a need to act, a need to tell her the truth . . .

"Get some sleep," he finally said. "I'll keep watch."

He watched on through the night while the ghouls in their droves marched into the maws of the dead whales. More beasts of the depths beached themselves for the purpose as the night went on, speeding the process. The pain of the souls—unable to fight back as they consciously subjected themselves to the murky, suffocating depths of the crowded bellies—caused his gut to twist into knots.

He tried to push it from his mind, tried to focus on the target, on Ubzlan. He was down there, somewhere in that town. Gazlan would finally have closure.

A few hours before dawn, the damned masses had dwindled to a mere horde, and so the Rose Squad set out. The sky was a black veil in the smoke, the villages were glowing infernos in the distance, and the green flash of necromancy pulsing through the ghouls was receding with the tide.

"How are we going to approach this?" Wutarl growled as they made their way down the ridge.

"Same as with the Witch Hat?" Merigol suggested. "Waltz on in there like a bunch of morons and hope for the best, eh?"

All but Gazlan laughed. He replied, deadpan, "She knew we were approaching. She could sense my necromancy and Wutarl's paladism."

"This necromancer cannot?" Merigol asked.

"He can, but he also knows of the living army approaching from the south." He gestured down the coast. "He knows that after dawn the garrison from the shipwright to the north will deploy to flank him. And he knows that his main rivals are across the sea. I imagine my necromancy appears as an anomaly to him. Instead of hiding in ambush, he is forced to move. We can smash into his rearguard, fight our way through, and smite him in the open."

"This is a bit rash for you, little necromancer," Wutarl said. "You advocated for mercy against the gnome."

"This is the kind of man who would slaughter his own family just to have more bodies in his army. He would snuff out the sun if he could. He must die."

Merigol cocked his scatter bow and ratcheted a joint on his exoskeleton. "Well, let's get to it."

Wutarl unfurled his new war hammer, Vinetta her new cudgel and one of her vines. Gazlan drew his mage rune scimitar and flourished it through the air—causing the blue markings to flash—and he prepared himself to use necromancy through his other hand.

"Are we ready?" he asked.

"Ready," Vinetta said.

The Rose Squad quickened through the thinning woods and brush. Green flashes of scattered ghouls swarming through the area perked at the sudden movement and swarmed towards them with a terrible rasping cry.

The party burst through the tree line as a horde hemmed them in from behind. Merigol pivoted and shot his scatter bow. The fanning cone of death perforated the rotting mass, which crumbled and collapsed as rank upon rank toppled over one another, crawling with terrifying speed to consume the living.

Wutarl swung his hammer into the air and channelled his paladism into the head. With a mighty roar he slammed it into the ground, and a wave of weak sunlight rolled over the swarm. The ghouls cried out and recoiled as best they could from the burning light.

Vinetta reached into the earth and found an ancient tree root with her druidism. It broke through the earth, forming a barrier between them and the recovering ghouls like a great serpent emerging from the depths.

The ghouls smashed into the great root, failing to climb over it as it writhed and bucked at their touch. They were blocked from the party, for now.

"Try not to use your paladism until we reach Ubzlan," Gazlan said. "We will need every ounce of strength you have to best him."

"Fine!" Wutarl panted. "For what little good my power will do."

The Rose Squad turned from the root barrier and found the fishing village laid out before them. It was built into a grassy plain between the beach dunes on either side of it. Beyond the simply constructed buildings, the pontoons extended into the ocean, where the slaughtered whales waited with open maws. Hordes of ghouls swarmed down their throats.

A smaller horde of ghouls turned and stopped short of the village outskirts. They thrashed and brayed—itching to rip and tear—but were held back by some invisible line. The necromancer who controlled them wanted the Rose Squad to make it that far at least.

"Hundreds of ghouls behind us or the twenty or so waiting ahead of us?" Vinetta asked. "Hardly seems like a difficult choice."

"Well then," Wutarl took a position at the front of the running group, "stay behind me."

He drew his axe, now holding the two ridiculously large weapons—the war hammer in one hand and his battle axe in the other—and smashed them against his breastplate as he bellowed an orcish war chant.

Gazlan summoned a cloud of dead organic matter around his hand like a gauntlet as he readied to fight with his new sword. He had never used a blade before, but the magic that pulsed within it felt natural to him. All he had to do was cut the dead flesh, and the runes would sever the enslaved soul without him needing to focus, easy enough.

"Are we stopping to free the ghouls along the way?" Merigol asked.

"We won't have time. Push to the village centre, kill Ubzlan, and they'll all be free," Gazlan said.

Wutarl cried out again and charged forth, necromancer, druid, and clockwork-enhanced bowman following in his wake.

Just before Wutarl impacted the wall of ghouls, Gazlan cast his gathered dead matter like a wave. The hyper-fast particles sliced through the first few ghouls like a scythe, and Wutarl smashed into the aftermath—bowling through the shambolic mass as he crushed and cleaved with hammer and axe.

They crawled over each other to attack him, but their unholy claws ricocheted off the blessed plate and caught in his mail uselessly. Vinetta was behind him, bludgeoning stray limbs with her cudgel and lashing out with her vine, which dismembered any ghoul unlucky enough to turn their attention to her. Merigol followed through next. He shot another scatter bolt into the churning mass to keep them at bay and clobbered at the stragglers with his crossbow, his entropic limbs strengthened by Wutarl's exoskeleton.

Finally, Gazlan dashed through the gap. He slashed and whirled and hacked at the tunnel of ghoul limbs closing around him. With each hit the ghouls cried their relieved death rattles and went limp, their corpses impeding the ones behind.

The four continued their charge into the tiny village, down the main street, and into the loading area by the docks. The dead whales were receding into the murky depths as the final ship readied to pull out, crewed by withered corpses.

Ubzlan the Necromancer stood by the gangway with three of his grotesques. These foul beasts were towering monstrosities, made of bloated carcasses and sporting many limbs at odd angles. They turned and growled at the presence of the charging Rose Squad.

Their foe—Ubzlan—was tall like Gazlan. He turned in a gliding motion, his long, smooth dark robes dragging along the coarse planks like a hissing snake.

Wutarl bellowed as he channelled paladism into the heads of his weapons and brought them down in unison. Double waves of light shot out from the ground and rolled across the distance between them and Ubzlan.

Ubzlan simply laughed—a sinister sound that echoed through his undead thralls.

With a flick of his wrist, he summoned a wall of dead organic matter between him and the blast. It hit the pulsating mass with red and green shoots of power, and then both energies dissipated with a wisp. Ubzlan whirled his arm and swept a whipping strike of more dead matter at Wutarl's arms, lashing his wrists and causing him to drop his weapons.

The same whipping strike continued past Wutarl in a dark wave. It struck Merigol's knee joint, breaking the exoskeleton leg and sending him tumbling over. Vinetta sprinted and skidded, sliding feet first under the dark wave of dead matter, while Gazlan leaped headfirst over it. He landed in a shoulder roll, quickly coming up onto his feet.

"It's over, you worm!" Gazlan raised his scimitar. "I am here to end your wicked ways."

"Gazlan?" Ubzlan said, his voice deep and fluid. "I thought that approaching power might have been yours . . . What have you done to your robes?" He removed his hood, revealing an aged Nunnadan face with short black hair, peppered with grey.

"He resembles you," Wutarl growled as he shook his wrists of the pain and grabbed his weapons.

The ghouls from behind them swarmed through the village gate but stopped at the loading area's edge.

"Of course I do." Ubzlan laughed. "I fathered the runt, after all."

"Gazlan?" Vinetta said. "You said your father was a druid!"

Ubzlan laughed again, holding his belly. "Unholy spirits! He told you that hippie was his father? No. He was just a weak man that his mother could shack up with to avoid my pursuit . . ." He cocked his head. "Until she didn't."

"You shut your mouth!" Gazlan cried. "You don't get to speak of her!"

"Oh?" Ubzlan recoiled with mock hurt. "But why not? I have looked after her this whole time. Something you or that druid could never do."

Gazlan paled. "No. Even *you* wouldn't turn her into a ghoul."

"No, you're right . . ." Ubzlan turned to the ship as the mooring lines were cast off by ghastly sailors. "Sweetie!"

A figure appeared on the deck and sauntered down the rampart. She bore the classic black robes of a necromancer and was younger than Ubzlan—about middle-aged—and sported long, curly hair. She was tall, slender, and striking.

"Mum?" Gazlan trembled.

She looked at him without emotion, and her eyes danced with amber magic.

"She's been bewitched," Wutarl growled, "by Nunnadan sorcery!"

"Very perceptive, *Orc*," Ubzlan sneered. "I would call you by your class and not your race, but from that display . . . can you really call yourself a paladin? Oh, and who else do we have?

A cripple and an elf bitch. Son, you have gone astray without my guidance, associating with weak people like this."

"I'll kill you," Gazlan said through clenched teeth. "I'll tear your heart from your living body. I swear if you don't release her, I'll..."

Ubzlan waved his hand, and the ring of ghouls around them swarmed forward a few paces before halting. "You'll what?" he teased.

"Do you think this is the first time I've faced insurmountable odds?" Gazlan stepped forward. The grotesques twitched in challenge, but Gazlan ignored them. "Do you think when Mother and I fled Nunnadan that we didn't wade through swathes of your pathetic followers? Do you think that when Grenery, my father—my true father—and I fought off your search parties for years that it wasn't dangerous? Of course it was. But I still stand. I am not some ember for you to smother underfoot, old man. I am the raging fire!"

Ubzlan cocked his head again. "Did you rehearse that?"

"Screw you!"

"No, no, I'm serious, I really liked it. Maybe I'll give you a fighting chance." Ubzlan waved his arm, and half of the ghouls arrayed around them fell over, dead. "Go on, entrap them to you. We will see whose fire is greater."

Merigol, Wutarl, and Vinetta shifted as the ghouls spread out to occupy the now empty spaces. Gazlan stared down his father silently.

"Oh, that's right. You and your mother had those morals, huh? The *old* ways. Hah! Pathetic."

"You're a perversion," Gazlan seethed. "I'll tear your head off! Release my mother!"

"Gazlan," Wutarl grumbled, "control yourself. He's getting under your skin."

"I'll release her if you ensnare one soul to its corpse. Go on, my boy, just one."

Gazlan twitched. "Release her!"

"Gazlan," Merigol said, "get hold of yourself. We can't pull through if you don't."

"Come here, Lilerna." Ubzlan beckoned to Gazlan's mother, and she sidled up to him, wrapping her arms around his waist and resting her chin on his shoulder. "Give me a kiss."

Wordlessly, she obliged.

Gazlan screamed and charged forward with his sword held high. The grotesques roared and rushed to engage him as the ghouls charged his companions. He heard the telltale click and splatter of Merigol's scatter bow, the crack of Vinetta's vines, and the bellowing of Wutarl.

He ignored it all and made a line for Ubzlan and his mother.

The first charging grotesque—standing head and shoulders above him—swiped out with a mutated claw. Gazlan ducked and stabbed its gut. The runes on the blade did their work and severed the bond between the souls and the monstrous form. It collapsed a bloated mess, and Gazlan leaped over its corpse to slash through the next grotesque, which toppled limply.

It was so much easier without having to chant and make gentle contact, he realised.

The third grotesque shifted out of Gazlan's reach and shot its claw into its own belly. It wrenched a chunk out of itself and lobbed a handful of putrid guts at Gazlan. He quickly ducked under the flying putrescence and rolled, scooping up a handful of dust in his hand which he pulsed with necromancy. He came up and fired the dead matter at the grotesque like a lance. It tore through its face, and it toppled over in a writhing mess, without a head or senses to speak of.

Gazlan reached the pontoon, panting. A horde of ghouls tried to leap from the ship, which was drifting away, splashing into the black waters. Ubzlan cocked a brow as Lilerna looked on with disinterest and amber, glazed eyes.

"Perhaps you are a raging fire, boy. The last time I saw you, you were this snivelling little brat. Now . . . well, except for the puny morals . . . you are your father's son."

"You're right. I am just like the man who raised me," Gazlan spat and flourished his blade.

"And you did not raise him in return when he died?" Ubzlan laughed. "How rude. Would you raise your companions if they fell?" He gestured behind Gazlan, who looked over his shoulder in a moment of foolishness.

He caught a glimpse of Merigol hiding behind Wutarl as he loaded his scatter bow. Wutarl had cut a swath through a handful of ghouls and had produced his whirring drone to rise and shine gentle sunlight over the skirmish. The repelling light gave Vinetta the breathing room she needed to conjure the weeds and roots in the village to shift and entangle the ghouls' ankles so that they could be cut down with ease.

"What a peculiar paladin you have there."

Gazlan turned to face his father. Ubzlan had closed the distance between them and was standing a foot from his face.

Gazlan screamed and swung his sword, only for his mother to leap into the narrow gap between them.

His stroke hesitated, long enough for the ghouls in the water to scramble up onto the pontoon. Gazlan swore and retreated as Ubzlan spoke into Lilerna's ear.

"Show them what you can do, my love."

She snarled and lunged after Gazlan in tandem with the swarming ghouls. She summoned a cloud of dead matter to her arm and launched it at Wutarl's drone, shattering the paladin's light. The drone spun away, darkened but still whirring in flight. The ghouls from the water surged into the melee without the light to keep them back.

The Rose Squad had barely recovered from dispatching the first set of ghouls and now had the second wave upon them. Wutarl bellowed and charged straight into them, carving a path past Gazlan's frantic duel with his mother and barrelling straight for Ubzlan, who looked on with keen interest.

Merigol's magazine of bolts ran dry, and he swore, bludgeoning the first ghoul to reach him with the butt of his weapon. His mechanically enhanced limbs provided him as much strength and ferocity as the crazed undead, but he had to pivot on his undamaged leg.

Vinetta traced a path in Wutarl's wake and assisted Gazlan. He was falling back under the flurry of jabs and slashes that his mother conjured from molecules of dead matter.

"I can't face her!" Gazlan cried.

"Take out the ghouls!" Vinetta answered. "I'll fight this battle for you!"

Gazlan broke from the melee and rushed to aid Merigol, who was quickly becoming overwhelmed.

Charging across the pontoon, Wutarl reached Ubzlan and struck him with hammer and axe. With the grace of a swan, Ubzlan glided around the blows, falling back along the pontoon as Wutarl smashed it to bits.

"Why not strike me with your light, *Paladin*? Are you afraid it'll be as useless as your initial attack?"

"I'll snap your neck with my bare hands, Necromancer," Wutarl roared.

Ubzlan dodged another strike. "But don't you feel betrayed that your companion is my son? I'm sure you have questions."

"He's displayed his good nature like you've displayed your evil. I will help him, and smite you!"

"You would see my way of things if you gave me a chance!" Ubzlan laughed as he evaded another strike. "Here, let me show you how I see things!"

He weaved his hands, and amber magic swirled between them. He clasped his hands around Wutarl's face and chanted in strange tongues.

"You . . ." Wutarl roared and then went silent, his arms sagging by his sides, the tips of his great weapons resting on the wooden slats.

Back at the brawl, Vinetta wrapped her vine around Lilerna's leg and tripped her over. Lilerna shot out a lance of dead matter in response, which grazed Vinetta's shoulder. With a cry she collapsed to the ground. A moment later Lilerna had scrambled on top of her, and the two became embroiled in a bitter grappling match. While struggling, Lilerna summoned her necromancy and raised the ghouls that Ubzlan had released, their souls still being close by. They twitched and moaned as they rose.

Gazlan slashed at the last of Ubzlan's ghouls and paled when he saw the third wave rising to shamble into the fray.

"I'll hold them off!" Merigol panted, having the time to load another magazine of bolts into his scatter bow. "You help Wutarl!"

Gazlan looked down the pontoon to see Wutarl writhing in the amber grip of Ubzlan. "No!" He charged down the rickety pontoon.

He was too late.

Wutarl's limp limbs stirred, and he turned calmly. He commanded his damaged drone to drift down to him, and Ubzlan stood atop of it. Gracefully, the drone lifted and floated Ubzlan out over the waters to the receding ship.

"You're exposed now, you filth!" Gazlan summoned another pulse of dead matter to his arm and massed it into a solid lance. He took aim at his father, who watched on unperturbed, except for a slight hint of discomfort from the paladism powering the drone beneath him.

"You'll get one shot, my boy," he called out.

"One shot is all I'll need!"

"Not if you want to save your friends!" Ubzlan pointed back to the village, and Gazlan stupidly looked again.

Merigol was about to be overwhelmed by his mother's ghouls. Lilerna stood over a defeated Vinetta, raising a blade of necromanced matter to strike the killing blow.

"One shot!" Ubzlan echoed. "Choose!"

Gazlan watched in horror as it all unfolded in slow motion. On one side, his father—the man responsible for starting The War of the Damned—was escaping, while Wutarl stood by bewitched. On the other side, Merigol and Vinetta were about to be slaughtered, with no chance that Ubzlan would free his mother afterwards. He would still need to fight her.

Merigol cried in fear. Vinetta flinched and covered her face.

The choice would break him either way. Achieve his goal and still lose his mother, or save Merigol and Vinetta—the woman he loved.

In a heartbreaking moment, he acted.

He turned from Ubzlan and fired his lance of necromancy at Lilerna.

It tore through the air—a shaft of darkness and green pulses of light. It pierced Lilerna's chest and knocked her back before she struck the killing blow against Vinetta. The ghouls about to overwhelm Merigol collapsed. Vinetta peered through her fingers to see her end had been postponed.

Gazlan collapsed onto his knees and screamed in agony.

Ubzlan laughed. "I honestly did not expect that!" The drone flew over the ship that was now fading into the fog of the coming morning, and he released Wutarl.

Wutarl grunted and dropped the drone. Ubzlan landed safely on board the ship.

"I'll tell you what, Gazlan!" Ubzlan yelled through the fog and smoke. "Meet me at the Dwarf Islands. Fight with me and the last contenders in this war. And you'll get another chance for vengeance!"

Gazlan rounded and bellowed into the sea. "I'll find you! I'll find you and every other necromancer who fancies themselves a tyrant, and I'll tear the life from the lot of you!" His voice cracked, and spittle hung from his mouth. "I'll make sure you all pay!"

"Gazlan," Wutarl mumbled, shaking his head. "What happened?"

Without answering, Gazlan sprinted back down the dock, past Vinetta, and skidded to his knees beside his dying mother.

"Mum," he mumbled breathlessly. "Mum, it's me. I thought you were dead."

Between the confused glances and pained expressions, there was a moment of recognition in her eyes. The amber sorcery faded, and she stared in disbelief, a faint smile forming on her trembling lips. She reached out, caressed his cheek, and breathed her last breath.

All Gazlan could do was watch in horror as the life left her and she slumped back in his arms.

"No," he whimpered. "No, no, no, no, no." He broke down over her body as the Rose Squad picked themselves up and gathered around him.

Vinetta held him. "Gazlan, I'm so sorry."

"We have to go," Merigol said. "The army is moving in from the south."

Wutarl gazed upon the columns of torchlight moving around the ridge on the coast and marching up the beach. "They'll think you are The Terror, Gazlan," he growled. "We must away."

"No." Gazlan looked up. Many of the ghouls still twitched and rasped under the coming morning. "No, I have to free the ghouls that Ubzlan still commands. I have to. I can't leave them here. They're in pain."

"There's no time." Vinetta squeezed him. "They will be free once we finish our quest."

"No," he said weakly. "No."

Wutarl dragged Gazlan from the ground. He did not resist. The battered Squad made for a dinghy tied to the pontoon. Gazlan simply watched his mother's body amidst the chaos as he was pulled along; she was all alone in the dead village.

They loaded into the dinghy and cast off. Wutarl pulled another drone from his pack and placed the propellers in the water. He tied it in place and charged it with a beam of light. It whirred to life, and the boat pushed away from the village and into the foggy dawn.

"I failed," Gazlan said. "I thought she was dead. I just went about my task slowly instead of going after her."

"You didn't fail, Gazlan. You freed her. She saw that you were free in the end. She would have been happy." Vinetta held him in close, rocking him gently.

"I could have saved her if I ensnared those ghouls," he choked. "If I had just used the full horror of my power."

"She would not have wanted you to do that," Merigol said. "It's like what you said about my Sinan. It would have been a perversion. It's why we're on this quest, to end this war and free those souls."

"I was always in it just to get to Ubzlan. I'm a selfish failure. And I let my own mother die!" he bellowed. "I lied to you about my family. I, I . . ."

"Gazlan." Vinetta squeezed him tighter. "This may have begun as a quest to serve your own justice. You may have hidden those dark secrets about your father. But none of us judge you for that. You have done much good. You gave us three here a purpose after our lives were ruined, took us in on your journey when you could have left us to wallow in our own failures. You have selflessly dedicated yourself to the hard path;

you have struggled to free the enslaved souls of the land. You put your own life on the line just to free one ghoul when we first met . . . I think that's why I love you." She leant in and kissed him.

He shuddered and tried to push her from him in his shock and grief, but she held on tighter. He finally relaxed and fell into the kiss.

She pulled back just enough to speak. "I think I've loved you from the moment I gave you my rose seeds." She placed her hand on his chest. "I think I realised when I mended your heart. Now it's our turn to save you. We will help you carry this grief, like you helped me carry the loss of my forest."

"The loss of my love," Merigol confirmed.

"The loss of my order," Wutarl growled.

"We are going to do this together." She embraced him tightly again.

Merigol sidled in and hugged them too. After a moment—and a prolonged sigh—Wutarl scooped them into a mighty bear hug.

"I love you too," Gazlan said weakly to Vinetta. "I love you all."

"We're family," Merigol said.

"A clan," Wutarl growled.

They relaxed their embrace.

"So what now?" Merigol asked.

Vinetta kissed Gazlan again and looked out into the brightening fog. She pulled Gazlan's hood down for him and caressed his head. "Now we end this *cursed* war."

Part VII: The War of the Damned

The dinghy chugged across the calm black waters that reflected the dazzling starry sky like an astral plane. Wutarl gazed across the two-tiered spackled majesty as he sat by the prop, wearily igniting paladism into the power cell to keep their graceful journey in motion.

Merigol sat at the bow, scanning the waters for threats with drooping eyes, and Vinetta cradled the sleeping Gazlan in her lap. She caressed his cheek and sang in soothing tones as fever dreams tried to claim him.

"How much longer do you reckon?" Wutarl grunted.

"The islands couldn't be more than two days away," Merigol reasoned. "Otherwise the village would have had better boats to get there . . ." He spotted a ripple in the surface of stars and tensed.

Wutarl sensed his tension, ceased powering the prop, and the boat drifted.

"What is it, Merigol?" Vinetta asked.

"I could have sworn the waters moved. Ubzlan must have many undead beasts in the deep by now . . ."

"Not just him." Gazlan rose from his slumber. "The ripple was but a tendril of the war raging below us."

"The creatures of the sea are fighting back?" Merigol gasped.

"We aren't that lucky," Gazlan said with a hint of wry humour. "There is a naga necromancer nearby. Sscrell. He has taken much of the Dark Seas. His threat enticed a coalition of necromancers to supplant his dominance before he overwhelmed the coast."

"Ubzlan moves in to assist his rivals then?" Wutarl asked. "He didn't seem the cooperative type."

"None of them are," Gazlan said. "Ubzlan is moving in to mop up the survivors." He closed his eyes and sensed with his necromancy. "The fighting is fierce below, and upon the islands not an hour away . . . I sense only a third surviving necromancer, and they are all fighting each other."

"Ah, to wade into a three-way war," Merigol chimed.

"Four ways," Gazlan corrected. "Many of the dwarves still struggle in the battle. We must hurry."

Wutarl breathed deeply and powered the propeller again. "My paladism won't be much use after this journey."

"Just leave enough juice to power my exoskeleton, friend," Merigol said.

Wutarl grunted.

"Gazlan," Vinetta still caressed his cheek, "are you ready for this?"

"No. But we have no choice. When I set out on my quest, there were dozens of would-be tyrants. I quelled many, and many quelled each other. I sense no other than these three left in the world. Whichever of them wins will be able to wage their war on the living uncontested; whichever wins here will become unstoppable. We have no choice but to ensure that none win."

"Then we will do so." She squeezed his arm.

"Vinetta, if I fall . . ."

"You won't fall."

"I mean, he won't be able to bewitch me because of my lineage. He'll have to kill me..."

"He won't get you. I won't let him."

"I want you to know that I give you permission to puppeteer my body."

"What?"

He held his hand over his chest. "You can use the rose that mended my heart to infiltrate my nervous system, like with those beasts when we first met. If I am turned into a ghoul, I could be used to summon my own ghouls in service to my enslaver. You must not let this happen. You can counter his necromantic commands with your druidry to nullify me."

"I can't take control of you like that. It would be unthinkable," Vinetta rasped.

"I would suffer any worldly threat to complete my goal. I would suffer any torment to my soul to protect my friends, to protect you," Gazlan said.

"But, Gazlan!"

"Vinetta," he kissed her, "promise me."

She bit her lip, looking into his dark eyes. Her rosy skin flushed as she considered the reality of what might transpire.

"I promise."

An hour later they sighted a dark presence in the astral reflection—land. It was surrounded by churning waters, pulses of necromancy, and flashes of resistance from the brave souls on the island.

"We're here," Gazlan said.

"Islands?" Merigol asked. "More like island."

"The dwarves are as industrious as they are tenacious," Wutarl growled. "When they move into an area, they liaise with the local races, in this case the water races. Here they filled in the waters between the islands to create narrow, artificially flowing rivers. They use them to sieve the minerals they mine for jewel smithing. They're also good for irrigating their paddocks for herds." His mouth watered. "Mutton."

"They irrigate with salt water?" Merigol asked.

"They have inverse towers which burrow into the earth and depths to mine the ocean floor. There is some mechanical trickery with pumps in those buildings to keep the rivers fresh while the ocean below is salty. I am actually excited to study it for my own tinkering... if we survive."

Something knocked the boat and set them to stumble.

"What was that?" Merigol darted his bow around the rippling waters.

"You don't want to know." Gazlan grinned even as his voice quickened. "Wutarl, more speed please." Behind them a titanic kraken tentacle lashed from the depths, enwrapping a leviathan beast before slamming back into the water. "Wutarl!"

The orc roared as he charged more of his light into the device, and the dinghy jetted across the growing storm in the deep.

"WHAT WAS THAT WHAT WAS THAT WHAT WAS THAT?" Merigol was screaming.

He raised his bow to shoot the titanic monsters when they breached the surface again. As they slashed and bit at each other with bone-rattling, concussive, and thunderous blows, smaller creatures that clung to their skin were flung with the ocean spray. One landed in the boat, an adolescent naga.

The child was marred by the foul arts of necromancy. It snapped and writhed to strike at the Rose Squad, and Gazlan gripped at it to release its soul.

The aquatic ghoul went limp, saved from damnation, but more slithered after them in the boat's wake.

"How can we kill the naga necromancer?" Vinetta screamed as she vine-whipped a murky claw that gripped the edge of the boat. "We couldn't fight in the depths even if those colossuses weren't waiting for us!"

"Necromancers of this power are extremely hard to kill by ghoul; they will need to face each other!" Gazlan bellowed as he swiped at a rearing sea creature with his mage rune scimitar. "Sscrell will be closer to shore where the fighting is thickest!"

An undead whale breached the frothing waters in front of them. The great mass loomed under the stars like a dark tower in the night and listed to crush them.

"Hold on!" Wutarl twisted the prop, and the dinghy drifted as it turned from the dead whale's path.

Another whale breached at their rear, jumping from the water to clamp its jaws around them. Wutarl bellowed another warning and turned the boat again, and the whale crashed into the waters, missing them by the barest inch.

A third whale breached next to the first. It was speared by the titanic beak of a lesser kraken from below. When the kraken wrapped its tentacles around the whale to rip it asunder, its innards spilled out, and hundreds of ghouls poured out of the guts. They swarmed over the kraken as it thrashed back into the waters, tearing its flesh apart.

"More speed, Wutarl!" Merigol pleaded.

With another bellow from the orc, the boat accelerated towards the approaching beach, which writhed in battle between the ghouls of many different races.

"This is going to be rough!" Gazlan grabbed Merigol from the bow and threw him onto the deck; then he threw Vinetta on top of Merigol and laid himself over them.

With a roar Wutarl channelled one final burst of acceleration into the prop. He dived on top of his companions as the dinghy slammed into the shoreline, sliding up the beach, grinding over the sands, and squelching over the bloated corpses.

The boat half screeched—half squelched—to a halt, and Wutarl was the first one up. He roared and swiped with his axe, dismembering a wide swath of the damned as they swarmed to clamber into the boat. Gazlan shot up and leaped over the bow. He slashed with his rune scimitar at the recovering ghouls and conjured necromancy into the dead matter in the sands to create waves and geysers to scatter the enemy.

Vinetta was right behind him, lashing out with her vines to keep the stragglers at bay.

Upon the boat Merigol struggled up and fired two scatter bolts in each direction. "Wutarl, I need you to power my exoskeleton!"

"I have no light left, friend," Wutarl grunted as he lifted Merigol with one hand and threw him over his shoulder. "Keep the fiends off our back!" He leaped to follow in Gazlan and Vinetta's wake.

As the Rose Squad pushed through the beach, they realised that many of the ghouls were not just swarming them, but each other as well.

"We're in the right place!" Vinetta cried.

They made it to the edge of the beach and pushed into dune grasses and higher ground as the battle raged behind them. Beyond the dunes they saw a curving river that had an outlet down the shore. A dwarf village was built around it, lit by the spackled starlight. The land had been carved into deep depressions around the curving waters; the dwarves had dug and mined and built their towers that burrowed deeper into the earth and ocean floor.

The inverse towers were a mistake in this conflict, as sea-based ghouls spewed from the surface floors. The dwarves fought a desperate battle on the higher levels as they coordinated a defence through interlinking bridges using the strength of crude firearms.

"This is absolute anarchy," Wutarl growled.

"Some still live," Vinetta gasped in awe.

"Ubzlan!" Gazlan sighted his father on the bridge over the river.

He had around him an army of ghouls and grotesques that were fighting off a stampeding charge of undead centaurs. The centaurs were commanded by a drow necromancer on the far side.

"The drow is Junla. Sscrell will be in the river somewhere," Gazlan said. "Let's go."

The party set down the slope towards the strange town. As they took off, a horde of ghouls from the beach swarmed over the dune and pursued them. Dwarves upon the rooftops and makeshift ramparts took notice of the approaching swarm and fired sporadically into the mass, causing it to crumble as ghouls were floored and tripped over each other.

"Do they know we're here?" Merigol shot a scatter bolt at a group of ghouls nipping at Wutarl's heels.

Vinetta flung her vine into the air and waved it wildly like a desperate flag in the dark. A shot pinged off the ground by her, and she almost stumbled to her death.

"No!" she cried.

"Wutarl, your light!" Merigol barked.

"I have nothing left," Wutarl grunted.

Wutarl cried out as a stray shot hit him in the shoulder, tearing through his chain mail and ripping his flesh. He did not falter in his step nor lose his grip on Merigol.

"Same side, you short, hairy bastards!" Merigol screamed. "Same side!"

The Rose Squad reached the first buildings and sped down the street to the bridge, where Ubzlan and Junla were concentrating the bulk of their personal swarms. The bridge was a haze of green pulses shimmering through the sprays of mist from whatever was brawling in the waters.

The dwarves above stopped firing on the sprinting party and instead focused on the swarm behind them.

"They've seen us!" Vinetta cried. "Finally!"

Gazlan pivoted without slowing down, skidding across the earth as he turned and sent a pulse of necromancy through the ground. The unholy green light shot through the street like a wave, gathering the particles of dead matter to roll and slam into the churning mass of ghouls like the tide against the shore.

Many ghouls were crushed as Gazlan reinforced the barrier, adding wave upon wave of dead matter for the ghouls to slam into.

Vinetta followed his lead. She faced the adjacent street where ghouls were pouring out of the lower levels to brawl with others. She reached down with her druidry and found coral lining the bottom of the artificial landmass and the towers burrowing down into the deep. She breathed her power into the coral and commanded it to surge upwards.

The sea life burst through the ground. It sliced the ghouls as she filled the streets, creating a razor-sharp labyrinth which they could not navigate without dismembering themselves to the point of uselessness.

Wutarl placed Merigol down and unslung his hammer. With a bellowing war cry, he smashed at the ghouls that rushed out of the nearby buildings—ignoring his gun shot in a battle rage. Gazlan and Vinetta continued their work, creating a stronghold within this section of the town.

The dwarves began to cheer and cry praise from the upper levels, but the lower levels still teemed with conflict between the living and the dead.

Merigol cried up to them, "Reinforce the upper levels! Get everyone you can to safety! We will kill the dead!"

"Aye, strengas!" a dwarf woman replied from the top of one building in her slurred accent.

"Sure, ya med besterds!" said another.

"What the feck d'ya think we've been tryna do?"

"Just do it!" Gazlan barked as he and Vinetta finished the barriers.

A grotesque troll broke from one of the lower levels, bursting through the wall before it charged at Merigol. He shot one, two, three scatter bolts into its mass to no avail. Gazlan, Wutarl, and Vinetta turned just in time to see it rear to tear him limb from limb...

Only it didn't.

It collapsed mid-charge with a collective sigh from the many troll souls that made up the grotesque, and skidded to a halt by Merigol's screaming form.

The squad looked around, bewildered to find that many of the ghouls surmounting or forcing their way through the barriers had gone silent. Much of the fighting within the buildings had died down.

"No..." Gazlan glanced at the bridge.

Ubzlan had Junla held down by many ghouls; he had just rammed a knife into her heart.

"This is good, no?" Merigol asked as he pulled himself away from the grotesque's corpse.

"Now the two remaining necromancers can raise these ghouls and concentrate the mayhem!" Wutarl roared. "We have to end this quickly!"

"How?" Merigol said.

There was a titanic roar and the sound of breaking foundations as the leviathan emerged from the riverbed. It was entangled still with the rotting tentacles of the kraken, and it slammed into the bridge, sending it crumbling into the murky depths.

The ground lining the river began to fissure.

"Wutarl," Gazlan said, "get Merigol to higher ground."

"I can still fight!" Wutarl bared his bloodied teeth.

"I need you to help Merigol and these people," Gazlan pleaded. "Your light is all that would help in the battle against my father, and you're outta juice!"

Wutarl muttered some profanity and lifted Merigol from the ground.

Gazlan glanced at Vinetta. "We can do this."

She nodded, setting her face in grim determination.

He flourished his blade and set off towards the crumbling artificial floor of the island by the river. It brayed and thrashed as titanic forces clashed within the depths, striking at the foundations of the inverse towers and making them tremble in the starry night.

They reached the last block of buildings before the river to find the ground had splintered and cracked completely, listing strangely like the shattered shards of a frozen lake. Ghouls of dwarves and humans and naga alike swarmed over the shards, desperately thrashing to find purchase as they killed and re-killed each other in the name of their terrible masters.

"Ubzlan could not have survived," Vinetta said breathlessly.

"But he did."

The leviathan breached the waters again and slammed into the breaking riverbed with a colossal boom. The minced head of the kraken writhed in its jaws as Ubzlan pulled himself from the leviathan's blowhole.

"That was close!" Ubzlan cackled. The deep reverberating sound of the leviathan cackling with him sent the remaining ground a tremor. "Ah, my boy." He sighted Gazlan and Vinetta on the bank. "Come for another spectacular defeat?"

"I have come to fulfil my oath!" Gazlan stood forward, ignoring the hordes of ghouls that broke from the conflict to stand between him and the leviathan. "I will purge you and all the perversions of necromancy from this world, tonight!"

"Gazlan." Vinetta watched as Ubzlan's ghouls were torn apart from the rear. They watched him and ignored Sscrell's forces, which were surging from the deep. "Gazlan, something is off."

"Well, there are only two more *perversions* for you to slay," Ubzlan answered. "You wouldn't happen to know where that naga worm is, would you?" He laughed. "The crossing was, hah ... eventful thanks to him. But I can sense him nearby."

He flicked his wrist and the leviathan shifted. Its jaw clenched around the thrashing kraken head, which gasped open, spitting a serpentine form from its maw.

"Ah, there he is!" Ubzlan hopped from the leviathan, sliding off its scaly head and plopping onto the wet earth. "Sscrell, my dear friend, how have you been?"

The naga writhed and clawed across the ground, making for the crack into the ocean.

"I would not do that," Ubzlan warned.

Sscrell's fingers gripped the edge of the crack, and an undead whale breached the waters; its maw opened and a horde of ghouls spilled out of it to engulf him. The naga spluttered and screamed as he was dragged to Ubzlan. He looked over his shoulder in panic, searching for his own ghouls, who were struggling to break through Ubzlan's lines, desperately trying to reach and protect their master.

"Sstop toying with me, critter," Sscrell hissed. "The moment my ghouls break through yours, you'll end me. Just do it."

"Ah Sscrell, you are no fun. I guess I'll just have to torment your soul instead, as it serves me forever." Ubzlan produced his knife and slit Sscrell's throat.

The naga sputtered a blubbering cry and fell limp in the ghoul's arms. His thrashing ghouls fell silent, the waters stopped churning, and the chunks of artificial land bobbed into each other pleasantly under the starry sky.

"Ah," Ubzlan raised his hands, "victory!"

"Not yet." Gazlan stepped forward. "There is still one necromancer for you to fight!"

"Oh?" Ubzlan's eyes flashed with green, and he sent a pulse of necromancy throughout the islands.

Sscrell's ghouls picked themselves up at his command, as did the drows. The combined might of three powerful necromancers were now arrayed against Gazlan and Vinetta.

Wutarl, Merigol, and the dwarf defenders watched on silently, barricaded above in their towers.

"Son, you won't even raise an army against me. What do you think is going to happen here?" Ubzlan said.

"I am going to tear your throat out and watch you writhe to death."

"That is a bit dark," Ubzlan laughed, "as in I can't see it ever happening. My legions will sweep you and your companions from the face of the world, your souls will be bound to your weak flesh, and you will serve me in perpetuity."

"Really?" Gazlan chuckled. "You'd just set your slaves on us? You would just flick your wrist and end the last *actual* challenge you'll ever encounter? Ubzlan the Terror, Ruler of the Damned . . . little bitch."

Ubzlan's head cocked to one side. "Are you trying to goad me, little necromancerling?"

"What master of the world would balk at a chance to duel his final opponent, a chance to demonstrate their right for glory over all?" Gazlan continued. "The Guardians of the Sun will one day descend to challenge your perversion, and they would first laugh at the coward who could not fight his own battles."

"The Sun Guardians will soon be no more." Ubzlan said slowly. "They are the perversions that shall be expunged, but that isn't something for you or me to worry about just yet. What you should worry about, dear son, is who the last necromancer you killed was. Did it make you feel . . . honourable when you slaughtered your own mother?" Gazlan gripped his scimitar, grinding his fingers into the hilt. "If you're going to goad someone, child," Ubzlan laughed, "make sure your own house is in order."

Gazlan growled and lunged forward, ploughing through the ghouls between him and his father. Ubzlan laughed and danced away while flicking his wrist. Tentacle tendrils shot from the cracks in the earth and entrapped Gazlan's limbs, holding him in place.

"Do you have any idea how many giant squid there are beneath us right now? It's ridiculous really." Ubzlan made a show of brushing dirt from his robe.

Vinetta bellowed her own battle cry and charged forward, summoning her vine to whip at the pulsing tentacles that held Gazlan and raising a cluster of coral around Ubzlan. He scoffed at her attempt as his ghouls surged around him, creating a fleshy mound for him to stand upon which rose in line with the razor-sharp coral.

More tentacles emerged; one lashed at her vine and ensnared it mid-whip as another tentacle wrapped around her waist and hefted her into the air.

"Let her go!" Gazlan roared. The tentacle gripping his sword arm constricted his wrist until the scimitar clattered uselessly to the ground.

"I shall, as soon as I have turned you to my purposes."

"Your sorcery won't work on me," Gazlan countered. "I may not have learned to master the power of the Nunnadan Shamans, but by blood right it will not ensnare me!"

"Then I shall kill you and ensnare your soul to your body. I will command you to rip this she-elf apart, and then I'll turn you onto your crippled friend and that pathetic paladin orc nerd. You can tear them to bits as my forces dismember the dwarves." Ubzlan lunged forward and swiped with his wicked knife.

The blade passed through Gazlan's neck with an accompanying wet cry. A jet of blood burst forth from the wound, spraying his father and his ghouls.

Vinetta shrieked as Gazlan went limp in the hold of the tentacles, choking without a windpipe. His eyes burned with fury even as they drained of life, taking in the leering face of his father, who watched him die.

He was dead within seconds.

The tentacles threw Vinetta to the ground. She grunted and gazed through tears at the forces arrayed around her and at Gazlan's corpse as it was discarded like garbage.

"I see you have feelings for my son . . . *had* feelings." Ubzlan approached her and she crawled back from his advance until she reached the crack in the earth with the deadly waters beneath. "It never would have worked out, you see; he was of superior stock. And you are just a pathetic elf druid." He reared with his knife to kill her and hesitated, then laughed. "Oh, silly me. I promised my boy that he would kill you." He turned back to Gazlan's corpse and raised his hand.

In a flash, Vinetta remembered her promise to Gazlan, remembered his words. He would suffer any worldly threat to complete his goal. He would suffer any torment to his soul to protect his friends, to protect her.

She raised her arm in tandem with Ubzlan and muttered her own chant.

She found the rose plant that had morphed into Gazlan's heart, lungs, and ribs, its petals and stems and thorns forming sinew and bone. The rose still pulsed with life, even though the body was dead, kept alive by the combined magic of paladism and druidry at its conception.

She spoke to the rose, to its final vestiges of residual life. She spoke to it and summoned the fungi strands from the stems and cracks in the leaves and the pollen of the flower itself to spread and seep into Gazlan's dead nervous system.

Then she breathed her magic into motion.

Gazlan's corpse writhed with a great spasm and picked itself up from the ground.

Ubzlan hesitated, withdrawing his hand. "I . . . I had not completed the necromancy yet?"

Vinetta bit down the urge to vomit as she manoeuvred Gazlan's corpse to face his father. She made it walk through the guarding ghouls, who showed just as much confusion as their master. The body twitched and limped forward like a deranged marionette.

"What magic is this?" Ubzlan turned from his son to face Vinetta. "What in the damnation are you doing?"

Vinetta's brow furrowed as she used her druidry to speak to the plant, which spoke to Gazlan's nerves. Her eyes shot open as she found the path forward.

"Forgive me, Gazlan."

She flexed her hand and sent the signal through the rose. Gazlan's corpse wove its hands and spoke a muttered necromantic chant, puppeteered completely by Vinetta. Through him she harnessed his power and cast the binding spell of soul to body—of his own soul to his own body.

The foul puppet shuddered as a flash of green shot through its body and gasped in terrible, wheezing pain.

Vinetta scrunched her eyes shut. She could release her hold over him now; he could now puppeteer himself.

Gazlan's eyes flashed with necromancy when he sighted his father and Vinetta on the ground behind him. His grin widened as the foul arts mutated his jaw into a fanged maw and his hands into terrible claws. He scooped up his scimitar in one meaty paw.

"What?" was all that Ubzlan could say.

"This is what you wanted, Father," Gazlan rasped, "for me to become a ghoul and kill something I loved . . . I once loved you." He shambled forward.

"This, you . . ." Ubzlan stuttered. "You are more than a ghoul . . . you're a lich! That's not possible! You need a totem of great power. You can't be!"

Gazlan's grin turned sinister. "The sinews of my heart have been formed by a rose of elven ancients, swelling with their mighty spirit. It was implanted by druidry, empowered by paladism, and beset in the descendent of the Nunnadan Shamans. I am more than a necromancer now, more than a shaman, or a ghoul, or a lich. I am your doom."

"Kill him!" Ubzlan shrieked in terror. "Kill her! Kill them all!" He turned and bolted over the crack in the earth and up the slope towards the buildings.

The ghouls and grotesques swarmed Gazlan, and with a terrible cry he went to work. He had now the ferocious lack of fear that an undead being possessed. As a thrall he swiped with the dreadful strength of one who pays no heed to worldly injury. As a master, he had the keen mind, skill, and wherewithal to dodge and block and evade. The first waves of the dead to meet him found themselves with crushed skulls or dismembered knees or were cut limp by his mage rune scimitar.

The undead Gazlan sprinted from the break in the melee he had created, scooping up Vinetta. He made an impossible leap across the growing gulf between the breaking land and the dwarf town. Tentacles lashed at them, and Gazlan swiped with his rune blade, stilling the creature of the deep.

Ubzlan made it up the slope and bolted between the buildings to find Vinetta's coral labyrinth had continued to grow and spread and intertwine the streets, blocking his path.

Gazlan mounted the slope and tore after his father with Vinetta in his arms. Ubzlan turned and shrieked for support as his ghouls swarmed out of the lower levels and into the street.

Gazlan threw Vinetta away when a grotesque gripped his shoulder and ripped his arm from its socket.

Vinetta was about to become overwhelmed on the ground when she heard a cry from above. Merigol shot down with his scatter bow in tandem with a volley of gunshots from the defending dwarves, and the swarm crumbled enough for Vinetta to summon more coral around her for safety.

Seeing Gazlan on the back foot with one limb, she focused her druidry, commanding the rose in his heart to grow and burst from his shoulder socket. His new limb was a thorned vine that twisted into sinewy layers and formed a deadly whip, equally controlled by him and her. Gazlan whipped at the grotesque, and the thorns caught in its flesh, tearing its head from its body.

He used this sacred yet unholy flail to batter the swarming dead away as he continued on his warpath.

Ubzlan was backed up against the corals as Gazlan sprinted forth. The necromancer summoned a smattering of dead matter to his hand and fired it like a lance at Gazlan's gut. It tore a hole through him and continued on after exploding out his other side, tearing down Ubzlan's very own reinforcements who had managed to evade the gunfire.

Gazlan stumbled and collapsed, heaving, from the force of the blow, but not the pain, though he could still feel it. But despite the pain, his master compelled him to continue on regardless... His master was him.

He launched up and wrapped his rose vine arm around Ubzlan's legs. The thorns dug into his skin, and he screamed as Gazlan dragged him closer to slice with his scimitar.

Ubzlan fired another necromantic lance, and it tore through Gazlan's chest, striking the rose. Gazlan's vine shuddered and went limp as he stumbled onto his knee.

Ubzlan scrambled onto his feet and conjured another lance of dead matter to finish him off.

"Not good enough, boy!" he mocked.

Then there was a bellowing. Wutarl charged from the lower levels, his weapons and armour drenched in ghoul viscera, and he roared as he summoned his last scrap of paladism. A beam of light shot through the hole in Gazlan's chest and struck Ubzlan in the shoulder.

With a cry and the sizzling of flesh, Ubzlan spun into the coral and got caught in the sharp edges.

The light burned Gazlan's flesh as well, but it also revitalised the rose. It pulsed and spread through his body as roots and stems and petals—intertwining with muscle and tendon—allowed him to move. He shambled forward and tackled Ubzlan further into the razor-sharp coral, tearing and swiping and dragging him through the snare.

Gazlan clawed at Ubzlan the Terror's face, striking at his neck and body until finally the screaming stopped. The swarming ghouls throughout the island fell dead with a sigh of relief that rolled over the land and out across the seas.

It was over.

Gazlan rose from the shredded mess that was his father and moaned into the brightening night. The stars were beginning to dwindle as morning approached. He dragged himself through the corpses to the side of a building and slumped against it as Vinetta rushed to his side. Wutarl and Merigol were limping behind her with a small company of dwarves.

The rose continued to grow through Gazlan, as did the seeds in his pouch, forming a garden of colourful petals in the earth around him which fed on his desiccating body.

"Gazlan!" Vinetta took his face in her hands. "I'm so sorry."

He grinned, a visage that was as horrifying as it was reassuring. "Vinetta, you survived?"

"Yes, and Wutarl and Merigol. You did it, Gazlan, you ended the war."

"Heh," he rasped. A beam of sunlight crept over the horizon and lanced through the street to fall on his face. "Oh?"

"We'll cover you up." She reached for his hood.

"No," he rasped, "no, the light doesn't hurt anymore . . . The Guardians of the Sun have witnessed me atone for necromancy."

"Aye," Wutarl grumbled. "You have done well, Necromancer."

"I couldn't have done it without any of you . . . but now I have to go," Gazlan said.

"No," Vinetta cried. "No, you can stay a little while longer."

"Vinetta," he rasped, "I'm in pain."

She scrunched her eyes shut and buried her head in his shoulder—in the thickening bouquet that was now his shoulder.

"But you are the last necromancer, period," Merigol said. "What about the haunted souls that need you to continue your work?"

"In time, more necromancers will emerge. I have freed enough souls for two lifetimes." Gazlan wheezed a laugh.

"So you're going to just release your own soul?" Vinetta wept. "Leave us here all alone?"

"I can't. As a ghoul I must protect my master at all costs, which means I cannot allow myself to die as I was the one who summoned myself . . . but you, Vinetta, you can override that with your puppetry."

"So I must be the one to kill you?" She sobbed.

"I'm sorry." Gazlan smiled again. "It is . . . a complicated situation."

"Oh, gods." Merigol turned away and wept. "I'll never forget you, Gazlan."

Gazlan's bed of roses grew more rapidly, engulfing his face as it decomposed before their eyes, his flesh fading to reveal his skull. His body became less, shrinking into bone as the soil and thorns and petals bloomed in the golden light.

"You would have made a good orc," Wutarl said. "It was my honour to fight alongside you."

"I will remember our time together fondly, Wutarl the Meek, Merigol of Frenk . . . Vinetta."

"Gazlan," she sobbed.

"I love you."

She leant in and kissed his bony forehead. "I love you too."

Then she reached into him with her druidry, talking to the rose again. She sent a signal through the plant, through the fungus, and into his withering nerves. The signal was a command to release the necromancy that bound a soul to its body. There was a pulse of green and a relieved gasp as Gazlan's spirit left him and his body sagged.

Vinetta stayed on her knees there, her head pressed into his skull as the rose garden claimed it.

"May the Guardians of the Sun welcome you into their domain a hero," Wutarl growled. "Vinetta."

"Leave me," she sobbed.

"Wutarl and I shall be there in a moment, if you need," Merigol said. "You once met me when our position was reversed. I will not abandon you now."

More dwarves emerged from their buildings, picking their way through the chaos.

"So, ah necramensah saved os?" one asked Merigol.

"Aye." Merigol nodded.

"We'll keep tha garden as ah sacred site. What was his name?"

"Gazlan of Nunnadan," Merigol said.

Wutarl turned to them. "Gazlan the Saviour."

Vinetta breathed deeply and rose from the natural shrine, turning to the new dawn with tears in her eyes. "Gazlan the Rose."

The Whim-Dark Tales continue in "The Daughter Of Darkness".

A note from the author

Thanks for reading Necromancing The Rose!

Your review would make my day! An honest review on Amazon or Goodreads helps other readers find this story, and keeps me writing books for amazing readers like you.

Want more?

Continue the story in **"The Daughter Of Darkness"** available now!

Visit **SEANMTS.COM** to:

- **Get a free eBook (and audio stories) when you join the community newsletter**
- **Read free short stories and articles**
- **Discover more books you might love**

Stay in contact on Instagram: @seanmtshanahan

Email: sean@seanmts.com

If you enjoyed this series, you will love my other books. You can find an up to date list on my site.

Thanks again.

Take care,

Sean

About the Author

Sean M. T. Shanahan is a Science Fiction and Fantasy author from Sydney, Australia. He is known for writing emotionally gripping, high-stakes stories that blend dynamic characters with intriguing concepts and take you through darkness into the light.

He has a lifelong passion for storytelling, and since publishing his first book in 2021 has produced multiple books that span Fantasy, Steampunk, Sci-Fi, and children's fiction.

Drawing inspiration from history, science, mythology, and adventure, he weaves immersive tales that will pull you in from the start and leave you wanting more.

Besides reading and writing, Sean enjoys nature, gaming, parkour, endurance sports, and making terrible jokes.

www.ingramcontent.com/pod-product-compliance
Ingram Content Group Australia Pty Ltd
76 Discovery Rd, Dandenong South VIC 3175, AU
AUHW012238300325
409054AU00002B/3